# *the* Timberline Review

## ISSUE 14 | 2025

*A publication of Willamette Writers*

| | |
|---|---|
| Editor-in-Chief | John Holloran |
| Executive Director | Kate Ristau |
| Editor-in-Chief Emerita | Susan Stecker Jones |
| Creative Non-Fiction Editor | Cathy Cochrane |
| Fiction Editor | Manny Frishberg |
| Poetry Editor | Sage Stanton |
| Copy Editors | Jakob Klein |
| | Martha Mitchell |
| Proofreader | Susan Stecker Jones |
| Readers | Madeleine Boyle |
| | Norris Comer |
| | Nathan Faust |
| | Stephanie Feldstein |
| | Dale Ivory |
| | Stacy Johns |
| | Milo Kashey |
| | Dana Mosher Lewis |
| | Nina Luther |
| | Martha Mitchell |
| | Deborah Mourey |
| | Ellen Shick |
| | Michelle St. Romain Wilson |
| | Melissent Zumwalt |
| Willamette Writers Office Support | Griffin Kittleson |
| | Kate Ristau |
| | Jack Wang |
| Cover Image | Kitt Patton |
| Cover Design | Lee Moyer |
| Interior Design and Ebook Conversion | Vinnie Kinsella |

Editorial Correspondence: http://timberlinereview.com/contact/





ISBN Print: 979-8-9864222-5-1
ISBN eBook: 979-8-9864222-6-8

## DEDICATION

This Issue is dedicated to everyone who helped see it through to publication — the folks at Willamette Writers, our wonderful volunteers, designers, and all the creative folks that had the gumption to submit their work for consideration.

# CONTENTS

# THROUGH LINES

*Letter from the Editor*

What does it mean to make it through, to see things through, or just be through and done? *Through* wears like a weighty but hopeful preposition while in the thick of things. Only after much has happened, having found a quiet, settled space to reflect, can being *through* take on some sense of closure. Seeking the perspective of time means sorting through the memories, returning to that unfinished state when one had to get through it somehow. The opportunity is to discover some pathway that connects before, during, and after. The arts provide traditional frameworks for arranging the pieces of life into something that tells the story, hence the value of visual art, poetry, fiction, essay and memoir.

When I agreed to take up the role as Editor in Chief in the fall, I had no way of knowing what it would take to see things through. The submission season had yet to open; there were volunteers to enlist. Well supported by the folks at Willamette Writers, the Executive Director, Kate Ristau, and past Editor in Chief, Susan Stecker Jones, I felt a sense of excitement mixed with trepidation. Submissions began pouring in, the window closed, and I had to turn things over to our readers. This year's issue appears thanks to the efforts of the many intrepid writers and artists who submitted their work. There is an existential risk involved in composing and submitting work. Putting things out there, not knowing how others will react, however, is how life works; one does one's best to work through it all. Organizations such as Willamette Writers and journals such as *the Timberline Review* connect people who might otherwise never cross paths. Looking back to those weighty moments of uncertainty, I emerge both relieved and immensely proud of this issue that you now have before you.

The selections that follow, though quite varied in topic and technique, struck a chord by presenting something recognizably human: fitting for our times and yet somehow perennial in nature. Feeling human can be harrowing—being drawn to the precipice—facing the unknown. Seeking meaning through writing provides a vehicle to reassure others that one is not alone in life's intimate struggles.

Richard Wilbur's poem, "The Writer," comes to mind, where a father describes overhearing the noise of a typewriter; his daughter is at work on a story. Amused at such intensity from so young a person, he wishes her well, but immediately senses her rejecting his condescension. Recalling a dazed starling struggling to find its way out of a room, the father reassesses his attitude.

> It is always a matter, my darling,
> Of life or death, as I had forgotten. I wish
> What I wished you before, but harder.

The contributions in this issue offer a timely reminder about the extraordinary consequences of ordinary life. Whatever life presents, compositions like these offer occasions to reflect on what it takes just to make it through. From the editor's desk of the *Timberline Review*, here's wishing you all safe passage.

John Holloran, Editor-in-Chief

# THE BORDERLINE JAGUAR

*Poem by Christopher Rubio-Goldsmith*

I

Many years later
your brother shows you the picture:
two of your tios wearing
black cowboy hats
under an October sun
in Douglas, Arizona. There they
are standing and grinning
in front of the Jaguar
      the green car strapped
down on an old flatbed.

(How good are any of us
at hiding things?)

Weekly they drove
      that same flatbed
with the classic
dark forest green car
on top like an old king
across the line into AP.
One-week new brakes
another time a redone transmission
then some slick rims.

(Few things in this world
cannot be counted).

That Jaguar never got off the flatbed
in Douglas. Even though
it looked like it wanted
to chew through the straps,
rumble up the Sulphur Springs Valley
to Bisbee.

In that picture my tios are young
and handsome with rebel stances,
their hands hooked into
their belt loops, their jeans
a bit frayed and faded.

        II
It was an easy task
convincing the other
because in Douglas when you are
barely old enough to drink
you probably ask yourself this,
"What is there to lose? Why
aren't we allowed
to speak those things?"

What happens when you only have
that one tired metaphor
and a pocket full
of cracked nut shells
and that old, busted watch
that reminds you
that time just goes on
and on—further than the horizon
over the hills
across that line

into a promise you might
make yourself and know
you will never keep?

Today you will just have to stop
being you.

# CAMERON GREETS THE SNOQUALMIE RIVER

*Nonfiction by Doug Emory*

I

I pull off the Middle Fork Road, nosing the car against the riot of blackberry vines, sword ferns, and moss-carpeted trees obscuring the trailhead to Champion Beach. From behind me, five-year-old Cameron shouts in impatient protest.

"Dad! Dad!"

I swing out, release him from his car seat's bondage, and dig his gear from the hatchback. I settle his backpack over his skinny shoulders. When I slam the doors, the sound echoes off the canyon walls hidden behind a forest of alder, cedars, and firs.

That sound sets Cameron moving. He ducks under a branch without slowing and charges through the trailhead's shadowed crease into the trees. His azure backpack bounces and his knit cap threatens to take flight. I sweep the branch aside and give chase. He's already nearing a bridge, its surface slick with leaves tramped black by earlier hikers.

"Slow down!" I yell, but that's a means of comforting myself, a pretense my status as father earns me some hold on him. He races over that first bridge and then another, this one a low metal structure angled through a bog. The gravel beach appears beyond that. Farther still, the river churns, a grey mass unspooling so fast it throws white flashes against the air.

I break from the trees and slow, sucking in a breath. The stones tip and give way, untrustworthy under my boots. Past the far bank, dragon's breath mist topples over the cliffs. On reflex, I reach for Cam's shoulder but stop myself. He's motionless at last, his toes bordering a shallow pool.

"Hi, Snoqualmie." Above the river's white noise, his voice is barely audible. "It's me, Cameron. How you doing?" His hand lifts to his chest, fingers bouncing in emphasis over his heart.

Those words and gestures are his mantra, our tradition. Cameron has introduced himself in just this way since the morning he and Snoqualmie became friends.

I respond with a chuckle deep in my throat. I play a role in this ritual too, my lines varying only slightly with the season. My voice sinks, turning gravelly as the riverbed: "Best friend! I'm good. Fresh snow in the mountains and lots of rain. Lots of power for me. Think I'll go flood those houses down the hill."

Cam's arms flap in exasperation. "Snoqualmie, stay in your banks! I always tell you!" Then, quick as light, his attention shifts. He stoops to work a stone loose. "You've got some pretty rocks today, Snoqualmie."

"Left them just for you," the river replies. "Take as many as you want."

I tag along as Cam chats and scours the beach. He applies a mysterious but tyrannical assessment of beauty to the surrounding stones. Those deemed unworthy disappear into the swirling water while those labeled beautiful end up rattling in my pockets. When their weight threatens to drop my jeans to the ground, I wrap an arm around Cam's shoulders and tell him it's time to go home.

His sweatshirt, heavy with his own collection of stones, trails his movements like a cape when he turns back to the river. "Bye, Snoqualmie!" he shouts into that onrushing wall of noise. "And don't forget! No more floods!"

After the beach, we stop at the Main Street Bakery in North Bend and pick up a box of pastries. I pass Cam a bigfoot sugar cookie and remind myself, at some future date when I'll become an efficient parent, to vacuum up the years' worth of crumbs ground into his car seat.

I choose the scenic route home, bypassing the freeway for state route 202 toward Snoqualmie Falls. Soon past the edge of town, a bridge's iron trestles loom ahead. I glance into my mirror. "Snoqualmie again," I say.

Cam spouts an unintelligible greeting. He shakes his cookie, and that mound of crumbs grows a little higher. Briefly weightless, we bounce over the bridge.

"Always happy to see you, Cami," the river growls. "Friend, come back to me again soon."

Minutes later, we're in the town of Snoqualmie with its train museum. The locomotives housed there usually stir a comment, but today Cam is quiet in the backseat. I worry he's stuffed the whole cookie into his mouth. "You need a drink?" I ask, but the silence stretches another ominous beat.

"Dad?" he finally says. Now his words ring, vibrant as struck metal. "Dad, does Snoqualmie really talk to me?"

My heart flutters. My mind fumbles through equivocations: do I confess, take a wrecking ball to the mythology we've constructed? Lie and delay the inevitable? Or—and here's an inspired third option!—do I dodge responsibility entirely?

The third option wins, easily. "What do you think, Cami? You tell me."

He makes me wait again, and the air gains weight by the second. Cam's voice starts low, then rises, convinced. "I think he does. He's just like nature. Nature talks, dad. Trees talk, so Snoqualmie does too."

I leap onto his answer: "Of course he does, Cami."

I tap the brakes as we navigate the tourist traffic surrounding Snoqualmie Falls. A parade of visitors marches ahead, one group after another disappearing into the mist thrown up from the cascading waters. "Don't tell your mom." I pass Cam a second cookie and give another glance in the mirror. "Hey, you want to stop in the valley and visit Snoqualmie one more time?"

He chomps out an enormous bite, then nods. I steer down the switchback ridge below the falls. In that oasis of calm while Cam munches and before the sugar rush hits, I pose a question to myself.

What would the harm have been if Cam recognized the river's voice as mine?

He'd loved the river from the first moment he saw it. That wouldn't change. But the prospect of his hearing me and not Snoqualmie shook me in a way I didn't understand.

I'm not naive. I adore the times Cam conjures a universe and pulls me into it with him, but I know the day nears when his ability to dream wide awake will fade. That change is natural. Freezing him in amber now would be purely selfish. Soon enough, believing a river knows his name, senses his feelings, and calls itself his friend will make my boy a laughingstock.

I drive on, suspecting my anxiety is spiking more out of concerns for my own evolution than his. Cam and I face a different situation than most parents and children, one that greets me each morning when my face appears in the bathroom mirror. At sixty-seven, I'm an absurdly old parent for a preschooler. Worse, I'm still too immature to view my son's growth rationally. Instead, I am focused on what the future threatens to steal from us. Snoqualmie's voice became the foundation of what hadn't been a simple relationship. How well will we fit, how clearly will we hear each other, if, as Cameron grows, the river falls silent?

At Fall City, I swing the car north. Cam tips his water bottle back and gulps down the remnants of his cookie. Where the river has undermined the pavement, the road narrows to one lane. "Dad, a front loader!" he exclaims. "Dad, a paver! A backhoe! Dad, look, that guy has a toolbox!"

"Uh huh," I say, "Uh huh." Fortunately, my ever-alert son fails to notice my thoughts run elsewhere.

II

When I told Cam he's a special boy, I didn't exaggerate. The fact a child chattered at me from a car seat was a miracle. His mom Joy and I had met dangerously close to the alarms set on our biological clocks. We knew a family might not be possible. We'd watched other couples ground to ruin by the failure of fertility interventions, so we cautioned ourselves against hoping too much. Early on, we set limits on the medical assistance we allowed and the time we dedicated to trying to have a child.

After another demoralizing trip to the doctor's office, we drove home without speaking. We walked out onto our deck together. The sun backlit the cedars, and they stood as black pillars against a violet sky. Crows spiraled in the distance, cawing as they prepared to bed down. Joy squeezed my hand. Our biological alarm had rung. Our timeline was exhausted. We'd fooled ourselves, pretending we hadn't hoped as hard as we had. The life we'd envisioned became a dream, and that thought strangled the words in our throats. The Fates had cut the thread.

Acceptance proved an awfully weak medicine, so, not long after the doctor's verdict, we leaned into the positive aspects of childlessness. We could travel at a whim, so we booked a cross-border jaunt to Vancouver. We splurged. The money we'd saved for diapers, bottle warmers, and a crib went instead to two nights at a chic downtown hotel. Our hosts provided their own wine tasting session, and, after that grownup activity, Joy and I stepped through the hotel doors onto Robson Avenue. The streetlights flashed on like a lightning strike. Crowds packed the side-walk. The air hummed with an energy fueled by dozens of interweaving voices, and we guided one another through a maze of bodies to dinner and a few additional drinks too many.

At five the next morning, Joy gave my shoulder a rough shake. She hovered over me. "Hey! Hey! Guess what?"

"You're going to the pool?"

"No," she said. "I'm pregnant."

She may as well have hooked me to jumper cables. "Let's get some coffee," I said. I yanked a t-shirt over my head and tugged up my jeans.

The streets were deserted now. Sun filled the skyscrapers' windows, and we waded through an ocean of light reflecting off the sidewalk. After a desultory tug on a locked coffee shop door, we strode ahead. We didn't have a destination. We listed and relisted the tasks that would pack the months ahead. The night before had been perfect, but it receded far into the past, just a sweet, frivolous memory.

A bedrock principle of mine is that I distrust unadulterated hap-piness, and I demonstrated this by veering between elation and terror as Joy's belly grew. Like a director plotting a film for the Hallmark Channel, I spent hours envisioning our son's first toothless smile and his tiny fingers gripping mine. I jotted notes about the cartoons we'd watch and the places we'd travel. Simultaneously, my sleep grew troubled.

I would wake in the three a.m. darkness and kick open a Pandora's box of age-related anxieties. Could I play tag without coughing up a lung? Invent games that held a kid's attention? Hear a child call in distress with my hearing aids out?

Not surprisingly, Joy's labor proved to be challenging. I trudged to the maternity ward snack room a dozen times, picking up juice for her and weak coffee for me. On one of these journeys, I bumped into a social worker who directly addressed the cloud of anxiety that trailed me. "You won't believe this, but you're lucky being older," she said. "You have a decent job and a sense of who you are. That's worth more than you know." Returning to the birthing room, I struggled to believe her assessment of me was accurate. Finally, after an ordeal that extended into Saturday morning, my fears crumbled into nonsense. Joy and I became the parents of a perfect eight-pound baby boy.

Cam grew into a beautiful toddler. Just the sight of him could break my heart with love. He sported a mass of unruly curls piled high on his head, and his eyes, sapphire at first, settled into a polished forest green. He was typically happy, but despite that cast to his personality, nothing was easy. Joy and I both had to return to work too quickly, so he entered daycare as an infant and immediately contracted the first in an endless parade of sinus and ear infections. His sleep patterns were as erratic as my own. He possessed an iron will, fought like a wildcat when being given medicine or having those gorgeous curls washed, and became a master at throwing tantrums, invariably in public places. Wailing in outrage, he would pitch to the floor, then go limp as a political protestor when I tried lifting him. I would decide to leave him for a foster family, then in the next instant relent and hug him to my chest. In a flat-out race, I could keep up with my little boy, but I never relaxed, always picturing him pitching down the stairs, toppling off the couch, or slamming a car door on his precious fingers. In these horror movies that rolled repeatedly through my mind, I never played the hero. I never arrived in the nick of time. I never discovered the magic wand that would soothe both Cam and me and serve as our go-to point of connection.

And all these deficits, I felt, were the result of my age, the unavoidable, unconquerable gulf created by the decades between his age and mine.

One weekend when Joy was away on business, I found a website about the Snoqualmie Valley Trail, which follows the river from the town of Duvall, up past the falls, and on to North Bend. "Let's go on an adventure tomorrow!" I said with forced exuberance as I tucked Cam in that night. The next morning, at an access point near the river, I unstrapped him from his car seat. He leapt out and launched into his usual mad dash, quickly abandoning the trail for a meadow filled with dandelions, anemones and yarrow beaten down by an earlier rain. He stuffed a fistful of battered flowers into my hands and took off running again. Steps before the trail reached the river bridge, I caught his hand, and we boot-skied down to the bank. The water level was low, with polished boulders still cutting the surface.

Cam's boots suddenly rooted to the earth, and he stared at the river. He hadn't stayed still so long since he'd learned to stand. His hand rose and his fingers made a steeple over his heart. "Hi, Snoqualmie," he said. "It's me, Cameron. How you doing today?"

The river whispered past. I waited for him to venture too near the water or sprint and fall face first to the gravel bank, but still he didn't move. He was expecting an answer.

"Oh," I started, struggling to conjure every detail I could about the Snoqualmie River—its length, depth, the extent of its watershed—but when I did speak, my voice wasn't my own. I coughed, deep in my suddenly phlegmy throat. "Hey there, Cami. Water's slow and kind of muddy. Too slow to be much fun." The river's voice was ragged with long disuse. "You know, nobody's talked to me in like a hundred years."

Cam stooped and pried a rock free. "I'm having fun today, Snoqualmie. I'll play with you."

After that morning, we scheduled regular adventures to the river. Cam's discussions with Snoqualmie unwound as naturally as they did with me from his car seat. They never ran short of topics. Some days,

Cameron carried a toy in his backpack for Snoqualmie's approval. During the height of summer, he would pause while kicking off his shoes and ask if the water was warm enough for wading. One memorable visit during the winter rains, we discovered Snoqualmie had flooded our favorite park, the picnic tables floating like tethered rafts in the dark water. On many trips, Cam mused about Snoqualmie's shapeshifting: the river arcing lazily past the sandy beach in Duvall, roaring through a mist-filled whirlwind over Snoqualmie Falls, and rushing, clandestine but inexorable, through the Middle Fork's shadowed forests.

As friends do, Cam and Snoqualmie checked in on each other's feelings. They offered each other advice. Both could be temperamental at times. Cam had learned, with his preschool teacher's coaching, to deal with frustration by taking calming breaths. Snoqualmie was always more circumspect about whether he could—or even wanted to—govern his seasonal kaleidoscope of moods, but Cam shared his advice anyway. If nothing else, a calming breath might convince Snoqualmie to leave our parks alone.

Snoqualmie grudgingly admitted to missing Cam while the boy was away. Lots of people strolled beside the river. Some even stopped to admire his beauty, but no one understood him the way Cam did. No one else wondered what he carried from the mountains, admired what he washed like gifts onto his banks, or asked how it felt to serve as the bus carrying the salmon to the sea. Loneliness during Cam's absences burned at him, evaporating him to nothing surely as flames in the trees along his banks.

"I'll come back tomorrow," Cam always answered. "Don't you worry about that."

My role in this dialogue never amounted to much. I followed along, one hand poised to catch Cam's shirt if he stumbled into an inadvertent dive. When we got ready to head home, I reminded him to thank the river for its time. Mainly, I marveled at how well the two of them meshed. They were always happy together, and when they were happy, they sparkled like diamonds.

III

Our final stop this morning is just outside the town of Carnation. The river murmurs, hidden behind a screen of foxglove and waist-high grass. We follow a sidewalk paralleling the water until Cam finds the secret path he's looking for, a track etched in the dirt. He shoves aside plants taller than his head, and for an instant he's gone. By the time I push through, he's already offering up a perfunctory version of his traditional greeting and sets off wobbling over another rocky shelf. Big-leaf maples hang from the opposite bank, darkening the river. Cam's arm swings, and a rock I hadn't seen him scoop up plunks into the water.

I saunter along behind. The boy moves like a Jack-in-the-box, dropping to his haunches every other step for some new treasure. From an expanse of apparently identical stones, he pronounces one and then another beautiful. His eye catches a stick curved in the exact arc necessary for his purposes. Without asking, I know all these artifacts will return home with us, stored in the trunk alongside those equally perfect samples gathered at Champion Beach.

I drop the stones he passes me into my jacket pockets then rub my palms together. The crusted sand drifts away, disappearing onto the beach. Something about the motion resurfaces the question Cam asked back at the bridge. I find the thought disquieting, like the memory of an injury I hoped I'd forgotten. Mornings like this are my last connection to our childhood dreams. They will vanish the minute my son says, "Dad, I know that's not Snoqualmie talking. I know it's you."

Cam sinks down and rises, another rock plunks into the river, and my feelings shift again. I almost laugh out loud. Here I stand, maudlin as a circus clown, overflowing with self-pity while the truth dances before my eyes. True enough, I'm an old dad. I've spent days considering how insufficient I am and how incapable I'll become. But Cameron entered my life with a river's force and swept me into a Dreamtime where rivers reveal themselves as gods. Through my son, I have been anointed to channel the words of a deity. Any dad, at any age, would be blessed by such an experience.

Cam heads off again, navigating the loose stones, his strides teetering but bold. A line of larger rocks has formed a peninsula jutting into the current. He flags his arm back, searching for my hand, his fingers slippery with water and grit. Once he knows I have him, he tip-toes that narrow pier to its end. The river pools beside us, its course momentarily broken, and Cam leans over that one still point as far as his arm can stretch. He peers through his reflection, staring hard at the being who speaks to him from beneath the surface.

## A FUTURE UNTOLD

*Photograph by Aliyu Umar Muhammad*

# SCRABBLING AT THE UMPQUA RIVER INN

*Poem by Tricia Gates Brown*

The occasion, Valentine's.
The ruffled skirt I bought
for the occasion. Trip planned

weeks before you told me,
not knowing we were done for.
I insisted we go. Brought

books, hiking shoes, Scrabble.
Wine I drank too much of,
tears cascading onto the bed;

on the Scrabble board: *TEARS*.
Connected at the "R": *MEMORY*.
Then the full arsenal: *END*,

*HATE, BETRAY, DYING*—words
I conducted on the board like a dirge.
You built *BYE, ROUGH*,

*REGRET*, and finally, *GO*. Adding up
points of our loss, we cut our trip
short, drove the direct route

home as I sang past swollen lids
and you hid your tears, face turned
toward the window. The withering

glare. Our last Valentine's.
Near the house, I stopped to feed
apples to our neighbor's old horse,

worried he could smell the grief rising
off of me, the way some animals smell
cancer, sense disasters before

they begin. How many days until
you moved out? Love ossified,
mirror-image of our fast love-falling,

when you were ever leaving, a pilgrim
at the border of love and hate. Your knapsack
packed with her mementos: photos

I would find on your memory card, in your
glove box, in storage. Windows into dreams
not ours, not mine.

# ELEGY FOR A CHAINSAW

*Nonfiction by Kylie Young*

## I. Wood

For my dad, cutting wood is a spiritual experience—with chainsaw hymns and tailgate pews, beer can cracking open like a Bible. My dad's Sunday best is a pair of Wranglers and a worn flannel. Cutting wood is men's work and prayer.

Cutting wood is spiritual for me, too—hell, that is. Whereas my dad revels in the work, each step rendering him worthier of heaven, I despise it. I hate the thick cuts of bark that scrape against my pale arms, the bugs that crowd me, and the pine needles crunching under foot on the uneven ground. I hate the way my body sweats and aches, and the way my low-cut bootcut jeans stretch against the muscles of my thighs, constantly slipping down as I bend.

But growing up, we relied on wood for heat. Each summer, we embarked on a two-week camping trip to the woods of Klamath County with the dual purposes of convening with nature and fulfilling our year's need of wood supply. My two least favorite things.

My dad planned his whole life around this annual trip, while I did my best to hide it from everyone but my closest friends. I was embarrassed by the labor. Or maybe I was embarrassed by the need.

My parents subjected my childhood friends to this labor, too, with their parents' consent, of course, and a share of the wood in return. By the time I was thirteen, we had the process down to a science. Wake up at seven, out by seven-thirty, and back to camp before lunch. One morning on that trip, in the early dew, my dad gently shook the side of our tent. It was time to work, quickly—before it got too hot. I donned my Goodwill jeans, my hand-me-down long-sleeved shirt, and an attitude I tried my best to hide. (Attitudes weren't allowed unless you wanted to freeze come winter.)

The crew assembled. It was me, my friend, my older sister, her friend, my dad, his brother and his father—four young girls, two middle-aged men, and an 80-year-old. Any real logger would have laughed at our gall. But we loaded up in the F350, which was adorned with wood racks made from two-by-fours scavenged in our backyard woodpile and drove down logging roads to a tree my grandpa had preselected. It was already dead, done serving its purpose in life and now on to serve us in its death.

After two weeks of work, our paltry crew had cut nearly 2 cords of wood. There's a picture of us posing with the wood in our work shirts and messy hair. The men stood in front of the scratched pickup, leaning with the pride of a hard day's work, while we girls, barefoot, perched precariously atop the pile.

We beamed with arms flexed, declaring *girl power*.

## II. Dirt

Cutting wood smells of dirt, that hot, sultry smell of southern Oregon soil cooking in the early morning sun. It smells of gas, dripping along the side of the red can like condensation on a Pabst Blue Ribbon. It smells of DEET and sweat and my first swipe of Secret deodorant.

I escaped those smells as soon as I could. By the time I was eighteen, we stopped going on this annual trip, girls grown and male bodies aging. I didn't live at home and didn't need the heat. My dad, uncle, and grandpa managed, somehow, on their own.

The last time I returned to those woods, it was me, my dad, his chocolate lab, and my grandpa's ashes. It was a quick day trip in and out to lay my grandfather to rest. We carried him in a small plastic container—the kind of plastic that bends under the pressure of your thumb—the kind you don't feel so bad throwing in the garbage when you accidentally leave it to mold. My grandpa sat in the cup holder of the scratched pickup in the armrest between me and my dad.

We weaved through the bumpy dirt roads, roads my dad could have driven backwards and blindfolded, pickup tilting with the grade. We stopped every so often, pickup running and dog panting, to spread his ashes in the river and grass. We found a clearing surrounded by trees and dusted the stumps with my grandpa's remains, giving him back to the trees that had sustained us, a gesture of reverence and thanks.

If my grandpa had had a choice, he would have cut wood to his dying day. Even as he lay on his deathbed, mind deteriorated from dementia, he mimed changing the chain on his chainsaw. "What are you doing, grandpa?" I asked, arms resting on the hospital bed's guardrail. "Getting ready to cut that tree over there," he stated, as if I were the one demented.

Back when I was thirteen, I watched my grandpa stagger under the weight of the wood, my teenage body staggering, too, but mine getting stronger as his weakened. I guided him to a stump to rest. He cursed his legs, which barely filled his two-dollar senior center jeans. He told me to get back to work.

I hated chopping wood, but I never doubted that I could do it.

My mom spent her youth tending to her own father's dreams of running a Christmas tree farm and building the perfect house by hand. I grew up laboring to support my dad. With two daughters and work to get done, my mom had retired from outdoor labor.

Obediently, I picked up a piece and steadied myself. My biceps tightened and arms shook from the exertion. I breathed deeply, inhaling the dust and debris I'd disrupted, and looked toward the bed of the truck, determined.

"Atta girl," I heard my dad say from behind me, wiping his forehead with his leather work glove and leaving a trail of wood flecks like a cross on Ash Wednesday.

I never believed what they said about Eve coming from Adam's rib. But in that moment, I knew it to be impossible. My ribs expanded to make room for my pride and lungs as I lurched slowly forward, in and out, right foot then left. My abdominals cradled my torso with a tenderness I knew could never have originated from anywhere but a distant feminine force.

Finally approaching the truck bed, I planted my feet, squatted my legs, and thrust the log up to my uncle, who was waiting from above.

I hated the work, but it felt damn good.

### III. Water

Each year, our camping trip took place over the Fourth of July holiday. There was no place my father would rather celebrate being an American than the river he had visited since he was a child. To him, our secret slice of BLM land represented the halcyon days gone by. A dutiful state worker awaiting his government pension, my dad lived out his pre-industrial fantasies in this two-week span each summer. He awoke with the sun, the scent of coffee and chewing tobacco slicing through the still morning air. He listened to the birds and warmed the fire as he prepared the chainsaws. He pet his dog while watching fish jump and reciting lines from *A River Runs Through It*. To him, these moments were more sacred than the church we attended on Christmas and Easter. But his quiet mornings were quickly interrupted by our girlhood groans, sleep stuck in our throat as we crawled out of our tents for work each morning.

After I threw the last log of the day up to my uncle, we girls returned to camp ready for relaxation. We braided each other's hair and played spy in the woods. When it got too hot, we ate popsicles and donned our swimsuits to float the river in old inner tubes, the black blow-up ones you buy at a gas station and patch with a tire repair kit—the ones that burn your bare thighs when you leave them in the sun too long.

My dad dropped us off two miles upstream from camp. After we'd floated about a quarter of a mile, the sky darkened and thundered.

Goosebumps rose on the section of my midriff exposed by my monkey-print tankini.

We weren't knowledgeable outdoorsmen like the men in my family, but we knew that you weren't supposed to take a shower in a thunderstorm. We helped each other dismount our tubes. I pulled myself out of the water, self-conscious about the way my stomach rolled and thighs squished flat. Soon we heard the truck return. We held our thumbs up like hitchhikers and slid our wet bodies over the tan leather of the back seat.

The thunder and lightning and rain continued throughout the afternoon and into the evening, the universe shouting as loudly as I wished I could have that I did not, in fact, belong.

We huddled in the trailer playing gin rummy to pass the time. A loud cracking noise broke under the apocalyptic purple sky. As it turns out, a tree had fallen by my grandparents' trailer right at bedtime. We squeezed ourselves into the safety of our makeshift trailer bed, sweat and river water lingering on our growing bodies, and our hair matted from dirt.

My eyes flickered open with each strike of thunder, catching the flashing silhouette of my mom by the window.

She sat awake, breathing in the rain shower.

IV. Fire

In the winter, we tended to the fire as if we were goddamn pioneers. My dad babied it back to life each morning. When I returned home from school, I stoked the embers with teenage ambivalence, hoping to resurrect the flames just enough for it to be someone else's problem. And my mom, who I guess hadn't avoided labor after all, handled its midnight feeding.

I often forgot my shift, realizing only as I heard the garage door open that I was, in fact, cold. As I poked the ashes to reignite the embers, I hated the way the fire grew then waned ever so slightly, taunting me. Finally, I'd provoke it back into existence, praying for it to absolve me of my negligence.

Our 1970s ranch-house stretched longer than our catalytic converter could heat. The hearth in the family room sweltered. My room, on the opposite end of the house, froze. At night, I lay under a heated blanket, face ice-cold above the covers. Clasping my hands in prayer, palms and hot breath warming my nose, I recited, "Now I lay me down to sleep. I pray the Lord my soul to keep. Guide me through the night, dear Lord, and wake me with the morning light." Then I cursed the fire and the wood that fueled it.

I paid my first electric bill when I was twenty-five. Before that, I lived in school accommodations and a basement apartment whose utilities were included in the rent. My new apartment was in an old green house in Eugene that had been converted into four units. It was absolutely shitty, featuring a faucet I had to turn on with a wrench and carpet ruined by other people's cats. It was also freezing. But it was $800 a month, had a clawfoot tub, and was, gloriously, all mine—exactly what I needed with my $1,300 monthly graduate stipend.

I opened the bill. It was $102.83. I called my mom in a panic. At her suggestion, I bought special cling wrap to seal in my windows and used my hair dryer to stretch it into place. I drummed my fingers along the surface, feeling the plastic succumb then resist, and waited for the apartment to warm up.

Not long after, when my childhood bedroom had turned into an office and my sister's room into storage, my parents finally had enough disposable income to fix the furnace that had been broken since we moved in twenty-two years prior. The HVAC tech helped them set up a digital thermostat, mounted on the dark green wall across from the bathroom. The ghost of our old, bulky, useless thermostat is all that remains, just a rectangle of white paint peeking behind the slimmer body of a new one.

I drive an hour north from my shitty apartment to my childhood home to revel at the new technology. I'm meeting up with my parents to drive to my sister's house in Montana for Christmas. We help out on my brother-in-law's family farm. My dad feeds the cows with my niece in tow, while my mom and I read to my nephews and watch the baby.

We haven't been back to our camping spot since we laid my grandpa to rest. The land has been reclaimed by the people who have cared for it since time immemorial, and we are, rightfully, not welcome. My dad doesn't talk about it.

The truck is old now. It's more scratched than before, on its second transmission. Dirt is caked into the floorboard and the door pockets collect old pieces of bark. It smells like dog and diesel.

I sit in the back, in the same seat I sat in as a child, squeezed in between the window and the graying dog. As we leave, my mom draws her phone from her purse. She opens the Nest app and navigates to the heat icon. With her manicured, bejeweled finger, she touches the screen and adjusts the heat down to sixty-five degrees.

Slow country music, the kind I've always hated, plays softly on the radio. My dad hums along, tapping on the steering wheel, while my mom closes her eyes for a nap.

The dog's snore rumbles beside me. I wedge my cold feet under his fur and rest my head on the chilly window, watching the Douglas firs turn into ponderosa pines and western junipers as we cross the border into eastern Washington. The dog sighs and snores louder.

I put in my earbuds to quiet the noise, like a good logger should.

# JOHNNIE WALKER IN THE THIRD DRAWER DOWN

*Poem by Colette Tennant*

I want to go back to my jazz piano teacher's studio
with one Starck upright piano, its high back
smack against the wall, like a suspect in a lineup.

I want my teacher to be there, waiting for me,
black hair swept back high on his head
full of more music than I'll ever figure out how to play,
his button-down shirt, tan forearms,
Camel bobbing in his lips, a PhD in cool.

His piano was the color of butter,
and the first time I touched the keys,
they gave in to my touch so smoothly,
I doubted the wood, blonde as any hero,
hid anything as harsh as eighty-eight hammers.

Out of a file cabinet full of lead sheets,
he handed me "My Funny Valentine,"
mimeographed paper muted as the blues.
The melody's single notes behaved,
but the chord symbols hung out just above the staff
like they'd just been let out of school.

All of it new to me,
a skinny teenager who, the morning before,
had sat at the piano in my little church
and played hymns from an ancient hymnal

with a spine so cracked,
it flopped open to Blessed Assurance
like an old bird with easy wings.

From his chipped coffee cup,
Dave took a sip of whiskey,
sat down beside me on the bench
shoulder to shoulder, elbow to elbow,
and taught me how to boom chuck,
tonic bass followed by full chord,
and how to lean into major seventh arpeggios,
soft as only anything new can be.

# SMAR

*Nonfiction by Rick Levin*

Motor oil. Dried sweat. Copenhagen chew. Engine grease. Salmon guts. Pumice soap. Pine needles. Garlic cloves. Old Spice. The scent of my grandfather.

As a child, I would breathe in that thick, heavy aroma like it was pure oxygen. I couldn't get enough of it. It was home to me. I'd make secret trips out to his workshop just to sit alone in a dark corner, squatting on a scrap of two-by-four, covered in sawdust, taking that smell into my lungs, letting it coat my nostrils in some childish hope that I could carry it with me like a talisman into my future life as a real man.

It was a point of pride in my family that we were Yugoslavian. What this meant, phonetically, is that we were "itches"—our people had names like Maravich, Babich, Jerkovich. This was exotic and mysterious to me. We were Yugoslavian immigrants. Our people fished for a living. My grandfather was a skipper, and he looked like all the other skippers we knew: an old, flinty man with a huge bulbous nose and dark olive skin, given to a sudden burst of Pidgin Croat.

"Hey, Ricky, look at that old *goolashava!*" he'd say, making fun of an old man, or "Hey, Ricky, what's for dinner? *Govno de schteckno!*" This meant shit on a stick.

And one day I too would become an old man like my grandfather, with an eggplant nose and sunburnt skin, lumbering here and there, visiting other old men. And I would give off that smell, because, in my mind, that's how all real Yugoslavian men smelled, like hard work, like a hard life lived.

Years later, after I'd become a so-called adult, given to bookishness and melancholy, I came across a passage in Faulkner's *Light in August.* He was describing the fictional Reverend Hightower's house, a lonely bachelor pad for a character who rarely entertained guests, and never women. With his particular genius, Faulker called the unmistakable odor that emanated from the reverend's house a *man smell*. Man smell. I shivered in recognition. I know that smell, I thought. I have lived inside that smell. And then I became very sad.

Nowhere was that man smell more pronounced than in the cab of my grandfather's Ford pick-up truck. As a child, I rode in that truck almost every weekend, just me and Papa, barely speaking two words between us as we rolled around rural Key Peninsula, which is the Appalachia of the Northwest, maybe greener and wetter but no less weird and wonderfully hillbilly. My grandfather drove impossibly slowly. We'd go here and there, eating up the hours. Errands. Visiting. Farting around.

On weekends we made regular trips to the county dump. These were the best times, the very best. We'd stop at the Arletta store—a real country store with penny candy and hardwood floors—one that my grandfather built long before my time. Papa would buy himself a tin of snoose and me a Reese's Peanut Butter Cup, which he'd set on the truck's dash. There it would sit in the sun until after our work was done. I'd watch it closely as he drove, the candy fluttering back and forth, making crinkly sounds on the dash, me dreaming, content, blessed. The world is a good, good place. I could wait for that candy. I could wait.

Sometimes we'd take longer trips, Papa and I, out into the hinter-lands of Washington State. We'd go visiting. On one such adventure, he told me we were going to check in on this old goolashava that worked on his fishing boat. "We're gonna go see old Smar," he said. For my grandfather, this was an excess of information, an esoteric hint about what was to come. It sounded legendary: Smar. I was excited, and just a tad anxious, because a smar also sounded to me like the name of some giant fish that that might crawl at the bottom of the ocean, something to be visited from behind the glass of an aquarium.

We drove forever through the forests leading to Mt. Rainier. It seemed to me we were driving backward in time, into a past where all the streets ran north and south and east and west and the houses were smaller, like model train towns, everything squared off. Finally my grandfather slowed the truck as we crept along an empty street of identical houses, either clapboard white or baby blue, none more than one story high. He pulled into a gravel driveway, nosing his pickup against the bumper of an old rusty car that looked like the kind of car a gangster might drive.

I know Smar was supposed to be a Yugoslavian like us, but to my kid's eyes he looked totally Italian. He had a big squarish oval head like a Brazil nut, topped by slicked back gray hair, his devious eyes resting baggy and hangdog in their sockets, and a sharp pointy nose under which he shaved a thin mustache. He was jowly, and when he smiled his lips curled and cut into his cheeks, so he looked like Joker on the Batman TV show I loved. He was skinny and loose-limbed and tall—maybe the tallest man I'd ever seen. He walked like a marionette.

"Hey, little Ricky," he said, stooping down to look into my eyes. "You want a beer? Whaddaya think, Sony, can the kid have a beer?" My grandfather shook his head in mock disapproval and tsk-tsked him. Smar cackled riotously, spit flying from his razor lips. "Okay," he said, tousling my hair. "Let's get the kid a soda pop."

I'd never seen a house like Smar's. It was plain and spartan, hollow like a church basement, completely unadorned. In place of art and plants and pictures it offered pure utility; a lone recliner, a ratty couch, a TV tray for eating and a bare television on a metal stand. There were Playboy magazines stacked on a dusty coffee table. I understand now that Smar was poor, but to my child eyes it was just another exotic place that offered certain information. This is where a man lives without women. It had the man smell to it, too, but it was a mustier version of it. The smell of a proud and entrenched loneliness. It made me lonely to be there, but it also thrilled me. A sense of possibility, of possible outcomes, fates chosen or not.

I sat there at the kitchen table, listening and not listening to them talk. My grandfather paid me little mind, and I reveled in this. He treated me neither like a child nor quite like an adult—I was something in between—and this gave me a great sense of belonging: of being privy to things I was shooed away from by my parents. Papa felt no need either to control me or entertain me, and I did nothing to upset the balance we maintained. I was little Ricky: a *dobra voltze*, a good kid.

Smar did most of the talking. He talked about the high school football team, and then, with a swishy, filthy leer, about the team's cheerleaders, to which my grandfather replied with a shake of his head and a glance at me. "Okay, Smar," he said, smiling. "Now now." Smar chuckled. You could tell he said it just to rile my grandfather up, and my grandfather was more than happy to play his role, the scolding Catholic. "Now now," he said. "That's enough of that."

We stayed an hour or two. We had liverwurst sandwiches and visited Smar's work shed, where he was building a new chair for his fold-out kitchen table. The old men stood around with their hands in their pockets, nodding. I put my hands in my pockets. I nodded, too. It was good work. It was going to be a good, strong chair.

On the drive back, my grandfather broke the long, comfortable silence. "Tony Smarovich," he said. "His name's Tony Smarovich. Smar." I could tell he relished saying the name, as though it were a bit of poetry, something to roll off the tongue and hang lovely in the air, like a myth unfurled.

"Tony Smarovich," I said.

"Smar," my grandfather said one last time.

"Smar," I said. I looked over at him. He was smiling.

Years later—after my mom got sick but before she died—it came my time to work on my grandfather's fishing boat. It was family tradition. My uncles had done their time, one by one, and me being the oldest grandson, it was now my time. I would run the skiff. And I was terrified. I wasn't ready to not be little Ricky anymore. I felt a dreadful apprehension about this new world I was expected to enter: the world of men, of hard and dangerous work, where fucking up meant something new, something catastrophic.

Smar was still a part of the crew. He was the cork man. His job was to stand at the stern with the other net men and pile the hundreds of yards of cork line that wound through the block overhead as we pulled up the huge purse net full of wriggling salmon. As skiff man, my job was to drag one end of the seine-net in a gigantic arc, probably a good half mile long, until Papa signaled to close it, after which I would bring it revving into the boat and rope off, closing the set. I was then hooked up by a lone line, either starboard or port, in order to drag the boat away from the current, to keep the netting from getting snagged and tangled under the boat as it was pulled aboard with its catch.

Early in the season I was caught out in the skiff during a patch of particularly nasty weather, trying like mad to keep the boat away from the net. It was hell. The skiff was pitching nearly vertical, heaving up and slapping down with a violent crash, wave after towering wave. The line holding the skiff to the boat would snap impossibly taut, making a squeaky sound, shooting seawater drops into the air before falling limp as another valley of waves brought me nosing down again. I fought like mad to keep the thing upright.

I glanced toward the stern and saw Smar gawking at me, laughing so hard he was nearly doubling over. He flashed me an expression of clownish abject terror—wide eyed, lips quivering, muttering aloud. He was mimicking the look on my face.

Later that evening, after the day's fishing was done, as the whole crew sat over dinner in the galley, Smar started laughing again. He looked up at me drunkenly under his brow. "Looked like Ricky was about to shit his breeches out there today," he sputtered, bringing a napkin to his greasy lips. There was something so pure and infectious about the old man's laughter that my feelings weren't hurt in the slightest. Instead, I just stared at him for a full second or two and then twisted my face into an exaggerated expression of pure terror. At this, Smar started howling. I thought he was going to choke to death.

Once he finally recovered his breath, Smar looked over at my grandfather, who was sitting there poker faced. "Hey, Sony," he said. "This Ricky's a good kid, dontcha think? Good kid. But he told me he's never been laid."

My face flushed hot. I sneaked a peek at my grandfather. "Shame on you, Tony!" he said, shaking his head. But I thought I could detect a little grin curling his lips.

Over the course of that season, I could flash that mock-terrified face to Smar at any moment and send him into a paroxysm of hilarity. It never got old, never diminished in its impact. It was a great comfort to me. Because, honestly, I was otherwise having a really hard time. I felt utterly inadequate and completely outmanned. I never once got comfortable with the job. I wanted desperately to return to childhood, to a time when I could ride along on the boat as a kid whose only job was to stay out of the way, to a time when I could snuggle down into the bunks in the hull, with its overpowering smell of men and work, its enveloping man smells, and nothing would ever change. Mom would never die. Papa would always set a peanut butter cup on the dash for me. And we'd go visiting.

In fact, I can precisely mark the exact moment I finally lost my innocence. We were fishing the salmon banks in the San Juan Islands. It was our first set of the day. I was told that we'd be close to a snag, and that I was to keep the skiff lined up with a near and far peak on the islands, like the sites of a scope, as a protection against the snag. My grandfather's voice was coming over the CB radio, but I couldn't understand a damn thing he was saying. It was just a garbled, staticky mess. And then I heard it loud and clear: "God damn it, I said keep away from the snag! We're gonna lose the net! Pull harder, god damn it! What the hell is wrong with you?"

My grandfather had never once raised his voice to me. Never. It wasn't just that he was yelling at me; he also had a tone, a depersonalized fury delivered with enough force to knock my soul from my body. Desolated. It was at once a realization of my worst fears and a severing of all illusions of safety. It isn't true what they say about fighting back tears. We don't fight back tears. We swallow them, and they drip down into a bottomless reservoir of grief.

After that, I limped around the boat like a sad puppy for a few days, heartsick, pouting. It's the way I respond to hurt feelings—with self-pity

I send up like a flare. Smar could tell something was wrong. He kept poking at me, but I was inconsolable. I'd crawl off to the upper deck after the crew ate supper and sit by myself, trying to hide on a boat with very few hiding places. There was a strange comfort in my sadness, of course, a comfort that I would grow all too familiar with as my life went on, as I progressed into an adulthood rife with the blossoms of self-pity. I did not love my grandfather one iota less. But now I was scared of him, too. And I was deeply, deeply disappointed in myself.

I carried that disappointment around for the rest of the season, as a kind of superpower. It elevated me. I wasn't any more comfortable or confident in what I was doing, but I was more focused. I carried that disappointment into the blinding fog one day, when I completely lost sight of the boat from the skiff. My grandfather sitting in the wheelhouse might as well have been an eternity away. I just kept the thing throttled and waited for Papa's signal to close the set, at which point I would nudge the skiff into the whiteness and hope I was heading in the right direction.

The CB suddenly crackled to life. "Close it!" came my grandfather's urgent call. "Close it! Hurry up!" What I'd failed to realize, and what I would only understand much later, was that he'd corked another boat. What that means, corking a set, is that you open your net right at the mouth of another boat's set, choking them off from fish before they can even begin to trawl. It's a vicious move. It harkens to generations and economic warfare in the Northwest fishing trade, an unpleasant tale for another time. It's not a particularly proud aspect of my family history, but there it is.

As I was furiously hauling the net back toward the boat, motoring the skiff through this misty cloud with no end and no beginning, I suddenly saw what looked like a huge ghost ship floating toward me slowly in the middle distance. It materialized from thin air, and now it was coming right for me. As it passed within a few yards of my gunwales, I stared up at the men towering over me. They stood unmoving on the vessel's deck. They were expressionless, lined up in a row, holding shotguns. One of the men put down his gun, picked up a hose, and unleashed a geyser of saltwater into the skiff, drenching me.

And then they were gone. By the time I got back to the boat, I was shivering uncontrollably. I glanced up at my grandfather on his perch at the top wheelhouse. A look of profound pity crossed his face, perhaps guilt. I didn't know which. He certainly didn't look angry. What I do know is that I was pissed. The relief at not being shot converted itself into a rage at being punked. I banked the skiff, and the crew tied me off on the side cleats and lifted me out. "Go dry off, son," Smar said, his voice flat but not unkind. The eyes he cast on me were sad and wise.

It took me hours to warm up. As we sat in the galley that night, eating supper, I kept silent. Nobody was talking about what had happened. Maybe it was taboo, maybe it was bad luck, who knows? Superstitions and ancient edicts rule life on a fishing boat. Certain things should not be addressed. I still don't know what those things might be. Maybe this is one of them—I mean this whole story.

I saw Smar nod his head at my grandfather. It was an urgent gesture, like they were playing cards, and he wanted him to declare suit. Papa looked at him and then dropped his gaze back down to his bowl of halibut chowder. Several minutes passed, just enough time, I think now, between the goad and the response, which was not delivered reluctantly.

My grandfather looked at me, a bit sheepishly. "You did a good job today, Ricky," he said. I didn't believe it for a second, but it didn't matter. They were among the finest, kindest, most healing words ever spoken to me, ever. Because these were not things men said to each other. It was as close to love as we got. It was more than enough.

"Thank you," I said. I looked at Smar. He was grinning at me. So I made the face at him, and he laughed like hell.

# BRIGHT EYES

*Poem by Christian Paulisich*

*Pinnacles National Park, California*

1
East of Salinas Valley, the rocks colossal,
igneous spire chimneys.
In the caves, big-eared bat pups
reared in darkness. We entered
the mountain's wet crack. Cool
light pooled where echoes rang
through each cavernous socket.

As daylight dwindled,
the boys played capture the flag.
Josh, a broad-shouldered football jock
a few years older, gave us nicknames,
*little boy blue, speedy Gonzalez…*I was
*bright eyes*, a deer in the headlights.
Like when my friend Ty told me he was gay
earlier that day, not to tell
the troop.

2
Eating voraciously by the fire,
I wiped spaghetti sauce from my pant leg
and Josh yelled out, *That's gay.*
A roar of laughter fed the blaze
inside me. In our tent,
that night, I wanted to ask Ty how

he'd known, how it felt to see
himself reflected in another body, a river
stirring, crystal. I turned into my pillow.


3
Even the tent judged me,
its flaps batting eyelids.


My troop agreed to meet for a picture
at the pinnacle where sun leathered
our hot and moist necks.
Looking up, I heard *Bright eyes,*
*know what time it is?*
                          Josh didn't
need my help though, having learned
to tell time from the sun. I tried
not to stare too long
when he caught me
that night by the showers,
the moon a glossy scar
upon my face.


4
One boy sang to the gray
barked buckeyes thick with lichen,
a great horned owl
                          by the filling station; another boy
streaked in the flashlight's strobe.
                          Once the rest left,
Ty said, *Yes, it hurt,*
but not as much as he'd expected.

## STANDING UP

*Nonfiction by Daniel Krug*

I sat across from a kid named Chris in second grade. He was proud of a medal he won in wrestling that year. It was the type of medal you didn't wear around your neck. He'd pin it to his chest on more days than not; you would be forced to look at it, silver and shiny. It would make a faint jingling noise as he walked. Chris loved to talk about how he was the best wrestler in his weight class on the island of Kodiak, where I grew up. He had to travel to the mainland to do a state competition to win that medal. He said he should have gotten gold, but the person who beat him was cheating. How could he possibly think anything else?

Chris would point to his medal, look me in the eye, and say, "This proves I'm better than you." Being that I was a poor kid who lived in a camper in a gravel pit, this stung more than it would for the average kid. Everyone knew my mom drove us to school in a camper van. Everyone knew my clothes were dirty, worn out, and too small. Everyone knew they were better than me. And lots of people liked to remind me. Especially Chris.

The island of Kodiak is big, but the town is small. The wrestling team in Kodiak was known for being one of the best overall programs in the giant state of Alaska. Kids from our tiny village and big island would do quite well at state-level tournaments on the mainland. Chris was no exception. He was a young boy with a bright future in wrestling. He also had the gift of wielding his pride like a weapon against the poor kid across from him.

Chris thought his words gave him power. He was a little boy who was super proud of his accomplishments, and all he knew was that standing on top of anyone made him feel better. Bullies like him don't even know they're bullies. They're just kids who are taught that respect is a one-way street. I didn't say anything back. I didn't argue with him about whether he was better than me.

I was eight years old, poor, homeless, and living with my mother and four other siblings inside a tiny camper van in a gravel pit. My older brother Zach was good at taking his aggression out on me and my younger brother. He was a lot bigger and enjoyed various forms of big brother torture to mitigate how kids at school made him feel, too. We were all made fun of. We were all mocked, laughed at, and ostracized for our dirty clothes and shoes held together with duct tape. Zach found lots of ways to make himself feel better. You'd think the shared adversity would bring us together. For Zach, it made him hate his family. He blamed us for how others treated him.

Given our location, we'd often just pee in the woods. Going number two was the only thing reserved for the toilet. So, Zach would wait until he saw me going outside the camper to pee, and before I could get my pants unzipped, he'd tackle me and hold me down. He wouldn't let me up until I peed in my pants. Then he'd laugh at me, kick dirt in my face, and call me a baby. Telling my mom wouldn't help. She would get upset at the dirty pants worse than the actions that got them that way. I'd often just not say anything and sit outside until it was too dark and cold, and I would quietly climb into my sleeping bag on the camper's floor near the door. By the next morning, my pants, though they smelled of pee, were dry, and I had avoided getting yelled at.

Holding his silver medal and looking down his nose, Chris told me how bad I smelled. I never said anything back.

During recess, lacking a friend's group, I'd play alone near the edge of the tree line. Back then, everything wasn't fenced off like it is now. We had trees and a forest next to the playground, and nothing stopped a kid from running into it. It was a perfect place to take a few steps in and disappear from the rest of the group. My imagination would take me down beautiful paths. I would see myself as a knight riding a horse in battle. Often, I'd imagine that I was a bear that lived in the woods and needed no one else. Bears didn't have friends. Bears were solitary and strong. Bears could take care of themselves, and nobody ever messed with a bear.

One day, Chris and a couple of his wrestling friends decided it would be good to come pick on the poor kid who hung out in the woods at the edge of the playground.

"Why do you play in the dirt—too poor to afford real toys?" He asked. Another boy kicked a small pile of sticks I'd gathered and used to make teepees or small structures.

Chris stood close to me while I sat on the ground.

"Kiss my shoe, poor boy." He stared down at me, his lips pulled thin, between a smile and a sneer. I felt tears beginning to push their way out. My eyes got hot, and my cheeks felt suddenly cold. The insides of my nostrils burned as I fought back the dueling emotions of defeat and defiance.

I didn't look up. "No," I said. I didn't want them to see my face.

In a blur of motion, Chris was on top of me, and I fell to my side. He spun, shifted, and got an arm around my head. Like an anaconda, his grip tightened, and my head felt like it was going to explode. He squeezed so hard that I couldn't scream or yell for help. I heard laughter. My vision had black spots in it. I'd never wrestled before, and I didn't fight back. Fighting back only made things worse with my brother.

Chris pushed my head close to the ground. The other boys kicked dirt in my eyes. Someone pulled off a shoe and threw it into the woods. More laughter.

"You ready to kiss my shoes now?" The words dripped from Chris's mouth like a disrespectful rich kid demanding service from a waiter.

I didn't say anything. I wasn't even sure if I could talk with his iron grip around my neck. Chris let me go and stood up.

As I lay panting, my view of dirt and roots was interrupted by a Converse shoe.

"Kiss my shoe, poor boy." The words hit like bricks being dropped on my head.

"Kiss mine, too!" Another boy chimed in.

"And mine!" yet another yelled.

Four shoes belonging to different kids stood in front of my face. I refused to look up at them. In my heart, I wanted to break their bones.

I wanted to crush them and watch them bleed. I wanted to make them pay for how they were treating me. I wished I could become a bear and tear them apart. I wished and wished and wished.

The ground was soft, almost wispy in a way. My tears made little dents in the dirt. Snot welled up in my nose, and I kissed Chris's shoe.

"Don't get your gross tears and snot on my shoe, poor boy!" He snapped and pulled his foot away.

"I-I-I am sorry," I stuttered, fearful of getting hit or kicked by the group. I squeezed my eyes shut and tried to will myself to stop crying. It just made it worse.

"I got a better idea." One of the other boys said. Hocking noises from his throat. Shortly after, I felt a glob of spit land on the back of my head. More laughter ensued.

The rest of them followed. I didn't move.

At eight years old, I was no stranger to cruelty. I knew I had to let it happen, or it would only get worse.

Once the spitting was done, Chris kicked dirt in my face. "Go find your shoe, poor boy," were his parting words as they turned around and ran back toward the playground.

That day, I went home and told my mom I wanted to join the wrestling team. Wrestling practice was nearly year-round, and I would have about eight months before the state tournament. My mother was happy for me. We went to practice, she talked to the coach, and he handed me a set of headgear, a singlet, and some hand-me-down shoes that were only slightly too big for me. They soon became my prize possessions.

Practice didn't start until about two hours after school. The wrestling mats got rolled out about twenty minutes before practice began, so I had a lot of time to improve. I ran stairs, did mountain climbers, and practiced the footwork the coaches taught. I spent hours upon hours working on how to step in for all the takedowns they showed us. By the time I'd been training for three months, I could take anyone down close to my weight class. Even Chris.

Chris rarely trained with me. He avoided me, make comments about how dirty and gross I was and tried to get others kids not to practice with me. The coaches often intervened and talked to Chris about teamwork and lifting each other up. They may as well have been talking to the dirt I cried on.

Every day I felt better.

The coaches saw how hard I worked, and it was obvious that some of them poured extra time into me. In me, they saw a fighter—a kid who had a fire in his belly and wanted more than anything to win.

I never talked about Chris or other kids. I never mentioned to a single person that their treatment of me at school had taken a different turn. Chris and his friends didn't physically attack me anymore, but they waged a campaign of words.

I was a poor kid. I had holes in my shoes. My clothes were dirty. I was gross. I used spit to wash my hair. Yep, I would not be allowed to forget my status.

But I didn't care what they said. When they talked about me, it made me work harder in practice and stay longer. Their words were fire. They only added heat to the metal I was forging into a blade. The treatment was dismissively cruel, and little did they know how much it no longer hurt but strengthened my resolve.

By the time third grade started, I was nine years old and had been practicing wrestling for a whopping six months. Despite that, I knew the coaches considered me one of the best young wrestlers on the team. I only knew this because we couldn't afford to pay the dues, and the coaches pitched the money in themselves to allow me to continue attending. I heard them tell my mother that wrestling was good for me and that I was a good example to other kids. The coaches wanted me to stay.

Third grade meant different kids in a different classroom. It also meant Chris was not sitting across from me. I still saw him at recess. He still kept his silver medal pinned to his chest. He still made fun of me.

By the time state championships rolled around, we had found a home to live in. It was a yellow house on the end of a street relatively close to the post office. The backyard butted up to an old Russian cemetery. The bones and detritus buried over a hundred years ago sloughed out of the hillside near the house. My father had come home from fishing and attended a couple of my wrestling meets leading up to the state event. He was proud of me and insisted on paying for my trip to the mainland—a few hundred dollars to cover my ticket and food for the trip—an extravagant expense for my family.

In the season leading up to the championships, I had not lost a single match. And not one time had I fought Chris. Chris was avoiding me, and I knew it.

After a two-day ferry ride and two full days of wrestling later, I made it to the final match. I was guaranteed at least a second-place medal. My family was not watching me, my coaches were off with the bigger kids from the high school, and I was getting the green band wrapped around my ankle by a referee.

"Do you have any questions?" the big, round-faced ref asked as he stood back up.

My singlet felt tight. I'd grown a lot and it was no longer loose in the chest. The veins on my 9-year-old arms popped out as they sat over striated biceps. I was not the same boy who sat face down getting spit on.

Getting spit on by the person across from me.

Chris was my final match for first place.

There are two bars of tape about three feet apart in the center of the ring. Opponents place one foot on the tape when squaring off to start the match. I looked down as I moved my well-worn cleat over the mark. I thought about the moment I had to walk around the woods near the playground to find the shoe they tossed out there. The way branches and roots dug into my foot and small bits of debris clung to my already dirty sock while I searched. When recess ended that day, I didn't go back inside. Clouds hung heavy and low in the sky, and I stayed out in the rain to wash tears from my face and spit from my hair. I thought about Chris making me kiss his shoe.

"Shake hands and get ready." The referee stood in between us.

I don't remember shaking Chris's hand. I just remember the ref's hand waving past my face as he told us, "Wrestle!"

I shot in, took Chris down with a flawless single leg, and stood back up.

Two points for me, one for him. I gladly gave up the point. I wasn't going to pin Chris; I wanted to win a different way.

The first round is three minutes long. The second and third are two minutes long. I wanted a first-round win by technical fall and that meant I had to get a 15-point lead on him before time ran out. Winning like this demonstrates exceptional superiority and skill over your opponent. I only knew that because my coaches said technical falls were rare and only done by the very best, because most wrestlers were too good to allow it to happen.

I would shoot in, get a fast takedown, and stand back up.

Shot. Takedown. Shot. Takedown. By one minute in, the referee could already see what I was doing.

By two minutes in, I was getting close. 22 to 11. Four more take-downs and I would have my victory. With ten seconds left in the first round, it was 28 to 14. Chris knew he was about to lose, so he shot in on me as soon as I stood back up. Grabbing my ankle, he tried to climb up my leg and take me down. I moved to the side, got a head and arm, and began to turn my body for the final takedown to win the match.

"Time!" The referee yelled.

I didn't get a technical fall in the first round. But I had one minute to stand across from Chris. Like a statue, I didn't move, I didn't avert my gaze, and I didn't care if anyone ever saw me beat him. I was a bear. Bears are powerful and don't need friends.

I was a Kodiak Bear, and I was going to tear my opponent apart.

The second round ended as fast as it started. It felt like Chris didn't even try to stop the final takedown. He was flaccid and limp in his defense. His spirit was broken. He knew he couldn't beat the poor kid. He knew he would never again be able to show off his silver medal at school and be proud of it. Not because he didn't earn it, but because the poor kid was the one that beat him.

Returning home, the ferry ride was different. Many of the kids who avoided me but didn't try to befriend me started asking questions. They suddenly saw a different person—a kid who didn't let the world decide who he was. And even though they didn't know exactly what they were seeing, they knew I was different in a good way.

When the ferry arrived at the docks of Kodiak, the entire town awaited us. My mother and father stood in the throngs of people waiting for their son to return. All the boys of the Kodiak wrestling team lined the edge of the ferry, screaming out to their parents. I took my gold medal out of the box and held it out over the edge of the railing, showing them what I'd achieved.

And, like a sudden joke from God, the clasp holding the medal to the ribbon broke.

The crowd went quiet as the medal fell between the dock and the ferry into the water below. I watched the water splash up and form a round ripple, reminding me of tears in the dust. Laughter burst out down the railing, and I could see Chris's smiling face as he pointed at me.

I felt like I was kneeling in front of a quartet of boys as they spit on my head again. Then, I flushed with anger and headed down the walkway towards Chris.

"I don't need a gold medal to kick your ass. You'll never beat me. Your friends won't either." I spat the words out in violent staccato. I turned around to walk towards my bag and found several older boys standing in my way.

They were the high schoolers, and all us young kids looked up to them. I stumbled back, but their faces immediately changed from hard to soft.

"Come here, Daniel." The state champion of the 165-pound weight division said to me. He touched my shoulder and looked down at me with immense kindness. Then, he held out his case with his gold medal in it.

"You can have my medal if you want." He said.

I hugged him. I could tell he felt awkward, but he allowed me to. I hid my face under my arm to keep the tears from falling out.

"That's okay. I don't need a medal to know what I did." My words muffled, as I kept hugging the young man who decided to show me kindness.

He gently pushed me away and looked me in the eyes. "You're a great wrestler and a real fighter. I'm lucky to have you on my team. If you need anything, you ask me." Then he looked up at Chris and his friends, and his face changed to something ominous.

"If I find out you're treating your teammates poorly, I'll ensure you never wrestle again." A sense of finality colored the tone of his words.

I wasn't sure if that meant Chris would get kicked off for being mean or if it meant something much more violent. I don't think Chris knew either. Regardless, it worked. Chris never said another word about me.

In the ensuing weeks, the coach got me a replacement medal and presented it in front of the wrestling team. He took the time to talk about how hard I had worked and how important it was to support each other. Everyone, parents included, had heard or seen Chris and friends laughing and pointing at me when the medal was dropped. Little did they know that moment would change their lives forever, too.

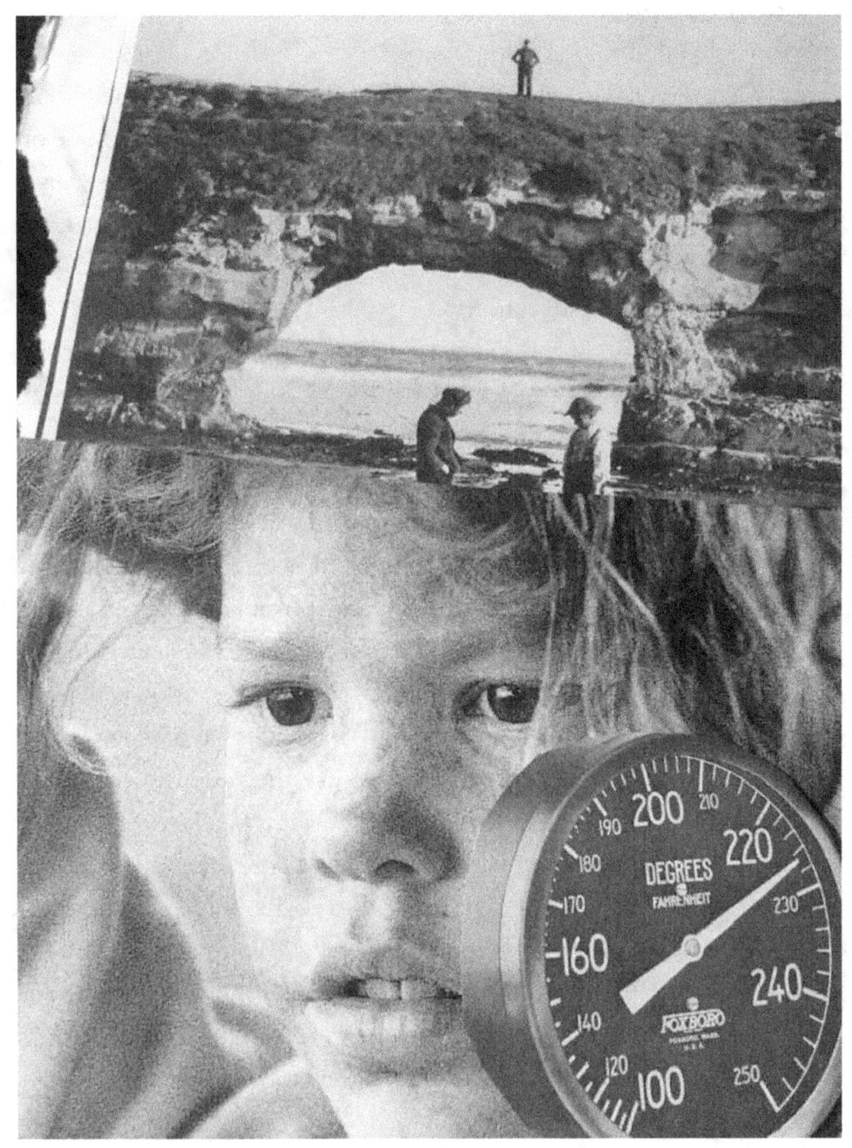

## DEGREES

*Visual Art by Amanda Yskamp*

# LATTES, LISTS, AND LUCY

*Fiction by Lisa Bishop*

Lucy twists the final to-go cup into perfect alignment with its neighbors and admires the symmetry of the drink trays. She gently places one on top of the other then hands over the envelope of exact change plus a fifteen percent tip. The barista calls out a standard farewell, but Lucy has already turned her attention to the morning staff meeting due to begin in seven and a half minutes.

At the glass door, Lucy shuffles her body around to press her hip against it, her hands occupied, balancing of drinks and extracting car keys from her purse. She has performed this exact feat almost every Wednesday for the last ten years without incident, always in heels and a pencil skirt, no less. Routines are delightful.

As she steps off the curb, a high-pitched beep warns of a delivery truck across the street reversing its direction. The harsh sound makes her flinch. The pavement of the parking lot feels miles lower than Lucy expects, and she stumbles. Coffee splatters across her car door. All eight cups of it. Well, seven cups of coffee and one tea, to be precise.

The coffees—and tea—are hot. Of course they are. But thankfully, due to the recent cold snap to hit Olympia, Washington, Lucy's arms, legs, and torso are protected by at least one layer of wool. Her gasp is more in response to the shock of the alarm than to any hot liquid splashing her.

Lucy closes her eyes, inhales, and turns a scream into a groan at the last possible moment. She will surely be late now. It's an intolerable example to set for her coworkers. She retrieves all of the debris, including the lid that almost rolled into the storm drain, and scurries back into the shop.

"Welcome to The Java Cave," a trio of voices calls out in practiced unison.

Lucy drops the used containers into the trash and rushes to the counter. She hastily dabs the square note paper, the back of her hands, and a spot on the left lens of her glasses with a handful of napkins. Once she is satisfied with her work, she moves the list closer to the waiting barista. His eyes are focused over the top of her, out the window.

"I need this order refilled," Lucy says, tapping the damp and stained paper. "Can you still read it?"

"No worries," the man says with the same sing-songy voice he used for his greeting. "So, whatcha up to today?"

Lucy is about to inform him that she will be in the restroom cleaning up, but she freezes, mouth half-opened. That is the same question he asked her thirteen minutes ago when Lucy first walked into the shop, when she handed over the pristine, more legible list of drink orders. Come to think of it, it is the same question he asks her every Wednesday.

"I'm going to work," Lucy answers. Again.

She watches as the man lines up paper cups, each labelled in black permanent marker. Beneath short sleeves, his tattooed arms and hands are on full display. The Tattoo Coffee Man—that's how she refers to him in her mind, though she knows his name is Cain due to the oversized name tag pinned to the front of his apron. He is packing coffee grounds into one of those little metal cups that twists onto the espresso machine. The lime green polish on his fingernails is chipped, not terribly hygienic. Lucy waits for the follow-up question she knows is coming.

She doesn't have to wait long.

"And what do you do for work?"

*Bingo.* Lucy narrows her eyes. Earlier that morning she told Cain she was an Office Manager. Last week she told him she was an Office Manager. Each Wednesday she says the same thing, because it is the correct answer to his question. She is an Office Manager. But he doesn't remember that. Doesn't really care, does he? Maybe the answer is a bit vague or too boring. But still, she spoke the words eleven minutes ago, at most.

A blast of steam whistles into a cup Cain is holding high around the spout. It is soon joined by gurgles. By the time the worst of the noise ends, Lucy has decided to give a different answer. Routines be damned.

"I work for a commercial insurance brokerage company."

Cain hovers a plastic lid over the freshly brewed drink. He stares at her, unblinking. Lucy focuses on the silver stud piercing at his eyebrow rather than on his eyes.

"Wha' didya say? A brokerage?"

His gaze travels over her face, drifting down to her chest before darting to her hairline and back to her eyes. Lucy can feel her heart beating in her neck. Her face grows warm. He is noticing her. Cain. The Tattoo Coffee Man. She doesn't particularly enjoy being noticed after all.

"Yes. Uh…" Lucy clears her throat and pulls her mouth into a smile. "Insurance. An insurance brokerage."

Cain laughs. Half his mouth—the half with the ring through the lip—curls into a combination sneer-smile.

"Oh, shit," he says. "I'm sorry."

Lucy bites the inside of her cheek.

"Hey, you can have my shirt," Cain continues. "If you want, you know, to change."

Whatever words this man is saying, Lucy has difficulty understanding them. This man with the green nails, in his dead-end job, wearing a store brand beanie. Are they required to ask questions and not care about the answers? Is she supposed to lie? Make up something fun, like film producer, in a futile attempt to impress strangers? She has a university degree and a stable income. It's more than she could hope for, except, apparently, for Tattoo Coffee Man to stop judging her.

Cain points at her chest. She hesitates a moment before glancing down. Perhaps he is playing some juvenile prank on her which will result in his flicking her nose. But it seems the issue is that her ivory cashmere pullover is adorned with a deep brown splatter. Cain's finger circles around her entire body indicating multiple incidents of staining.

"There's whipped cream in your hair, too," he says. "You should go get cleaned up while I finish the drinks. Bathrooms are right over there."

Lucy takes a deep breath. She tries to smile again but can't quite muster the motivation for it. She knows perfectly well where the restrooms are. Halfway there, Cain calls out.

"What about my shirt? I swear you can borrow it. I don't need it today. And it'd be great advertising for us."

Lucy can't wear one of the ridiculous Java Cave polo shirts into the office. She shakes her head, failing to say words out loud as Cain walks around the counter.

"Here. It might not fit, but at least it's dry." He holds out a wad of purple and orange fabric. "And clean. I think."

Cain sniffs the shirt, grins, and thrusts it back toward Lucy. Not the store polo, it looks like a rag used to clean a child's hands after finger painting.

"I…I can't," Lucy says. "I can't wear that to work."

"You can't wear *that* to work, can you? Probably feels nasty. Here, take it. It's my band. Do you like punk rock? We play sometimes at Mud Castles. You should come."

Lucy takes the t-shirt, simply to end the conversation. She has no intention of putting it on her body. She will clean her sweater. She will get the whipped cream out of her hair. Then she will get on with the business at hand. Coffee, work, staff meeting, routine.

Eight minutes later, Lucy stares at her reflection in the mirror. She's more of a mess than when she entered. Surely no one will take her seriously at the office when she looks like this. She has rinsed out her hair, and the curls are thickening into knots with each passing second. It will soon be impossible to return it to a tidy twist. Her skirt and tights are stained, but their dark color hides it well.

The sweater her parents gave her for Christmas last month is a total loss. The more she tries to rinse out the stain, the more it spreads. Cashmere can't get wet. Not without stiffening, shrinking, and warping beyond recovery. If only she'd remembered that fact four and half minutes ago.

Lucy drops the sweater in the trash bin and sighs. On her body is a purple and orange tie-dyed t-shirt with the words *Wagging Tungz* emblazoned on the back. The black letters are five inches tall and shaped like stylized tongues, seemingly performing tongue-like maneuvers on their neighbors. The short sleeves hit Lucy below the elbows. The bottom hem nears her knees.

She looks young and small. Five foot two isn't that short. At age thirty-two Lucy isn't that young anymore, but her lack of curves causes most people to mistake her for a child. To counteract this, she wears high heels, always. She meticulously applies make-up and wraps her hair into very adult-looking styles. All to look her most professional. Like a woman. An adult, college educated, professional woman, currently wearing the most juvenile t-shirt ever made.

Lucy spends several more minutes folding pleats into the shirt and wrapping her belt around the outside to hold it in place. That successfully hides the worst of the graphics. She secures her hair off her face but leaves it hanging down her back in an attempt to hide the letters still on display.

She starts to dig her phone out of her purse. Her coworkers are probably worried sick. A knock on the door interrupts her.

"You good in there?" Cain calls out.

*No.*

If Lucy opens her mouth, she will scream, or cry. She turns away from the mirror and cracks the door open. That way he can see she is still alive.

"Okay?" Cain asks. "How's the shirt?"

"Too loose."

Lucy's voice falters. Cain presses his face against the door frame.

"Better than tight and fussy."

Lucy frowns. This man simply cannot understand how important a dignified image is to being successful in the workplace. He earns a minimum wage for watching milk steam and dreams of rock band grandeur, and he looks like it.

"It's not professional," she says.

"You look comfortable."

Despite her work wardrobe, Lucy does appreciate comfort. She simply limits it to the privacy of her home. The office will think she's lost her mind when she shows up in such casual attire.

"Are you any good at your job?" Cain asks.

"Of course I am. What kind of question is that?"

"Listen. I'm a musician, right? I gotta get on stage and perform. Just like you're gonna do at work today. Stage fright. I get that. But it's only the first couple seconds. Then it comes down to skill and attitude. Have some confidence about it. If you act like the shirt is your style, no one's going to question it."

Lucy admits to herself that Cain has a point. Attitude. Confidence. Yes, she is good at her job. Really, no one seems to pay any attention to her on a normal day, so why would they notice this shirt? She rolls her shoulders back with a deep breath.

"Hell yeah," Cain says when Lucy emerges from the restroom. She follows him back to the counter. "You look ruckin'. Purple really makes your eyes pop. And, God, your hair is—"

Instinctively, Lucy reaches up to smooth the frizz around her face. She's never heard the term *rucking*, but she knows exactly what her hair looks like.

"—titanic. Wear it down. Unhook it. Let's see it all wild and—"

"Are the drinks finished?" Lucy's voice might be too loud.

"Right over here. I'll carry them out for you, just in case."

"That won't be necess—"

Lucy sees the list resting on top of the cups. The paper has dried into a crinkled lump. The ink has bled into a single splotch. There is a gap across two of the names where the paper has torn away.

"You can't read that," she says. "How are these orders even close to being correct?"

Cain crosses his arms. His fingers twitch a rhythm against his ribcage, but he is still grinning.

"Two vanillas with whole milk," he says, "a sugar-free caramel, a Mocha Mint Madness with chocolate drizzle, two hazelnut soys—both with whipped cream but only one with a dust of cinnamon. And a chai tea latte with coconut milk. All sixteen ounces. Same thing every week. Except for Rose. Never the same order. That lady's kooky."

"Kooky?" Lucy would take offense on her co-worker's behalf except for Cain's smile. He seems to be admiring Rose.

"Today she wanted Lavender-Raspberry-Pumpkin Spice with hemp milk. She won't like it."

Every Tuesday evening before leaving the office, Lucy writes out the drink list for the following day's staff meeting. She walks to each desk with a four-by-four inch piece of paper. Everyone except Rose orders the exact same drink as the week before, but she verifies them all the same. That's respectful. Even so, Lucy would not be able to recite the list as Cain did. That is why lists are made. She will simply have to trust that his memory is adequate.

"Very well," she says. "Though if you remember orders so well, why did you ask about my job as if you'd forgotten?"

"Standard protocol. I wouldn't mind changing it up a bit, personally. Besides, you like Wednesdays to be the same, don't you? You always seemed so proud when you got to tell me you're an office manager."

Cain sets one tray on top of the other and picks up the stack. Lucy was—is—proud of her job. And she does like her Wednesdays to be the same, or she thought she had. She holds the doors open. Cain sets the trays on the floor behind her driver's seat. The sticky mess has been cleaned off her car. Lucy asks if he took care of that, too.

"Mallone did it."

"Thank Mallone for me. You have all gone above and beyond for me today."

"No worries," Cain says. "It sucks to have a bad day."

"Oh, I haven't paid you for the second round."

Somehow, every event following a disruption in routine gets pushed out of its efficient shape as well, like forgetting to abide by laws and pay for drink orders.

"Manager says this one's on the house."

"Nonsense. Tell your manager it was all my fault, and the company needs its money."

Cain tilts his head and frowns up at the crisp morning sky as if listening to a voice from far away.

"Manager says he doesn't care about the money. Only that the customer has a better day."

Lucy is confused. Experience tells her she has stared at Cain too long, but she needs the extra time to process all her thoughts about protocols and chipped nail polish and dead-end jobs. Cain chuckles.

"I'm the manager, Lucy," he says. "I've decided you don't have to pay this time. My tips will cover it."

The man can't possibly earn enough in tips each day, considering the hefty expense of Lucy's order. She pays a tip as expected, but she assumes most other customers don't bother. Her face begins to hurt from her frowning.

"I can tell you have questions," Cain says. "I'll fill you in, okay? I get on average three hundred bucks in tips each week. I'm hourly, and so yes, I'm allowed tips. I'm the *shift* manager which is a glorified babysitter, and I got promoted to that because I've worked here the longest. Five years, in case you can't remember."

Lucy could not remember. The Tattoo Coffee Man had at some point in time taken the place of Girl Who Sucks on Her Teeth who had shown up shortly after Grumpy Old Dude with Mustache. Lucy has quarterly reports, purchase orders, and updated marketing strategies occupying her mind on any given Wednesday. She is mildly aware of Dancing Drive-thru Lady and Thin Blonde Cashier, one of whom is presumably Mallone.

For five years Cain has made eight drinks for her. He has smiled jauntily on every occasion, as if he enjoys the work. It explains knowing her list so well. Shame oozes into Lucy's belly.

"I apologize, Cain," she says. "I have clearly not paid as much attention to you as…wait, you know my name?"

He called her Lucy. She has never told him her name. She has never said more than ten words to the man before today. He sees a list of eight names each week, but she could be any of them. She could be kooky Rose.

"No, you pay tons of attention," Cain says. "Calculating exact change every week? Who does that? And you show up a couple minutes after the commute rush clears out. That's either damn perfect coincidence or planned after years of observation."

"It's only efficient." Lucy changed the staff meeting start time eight years ago by twenty minutes to accommodate her coffee stop. No one else ever arrived promptly anyway.

"It's also considerate. And I know you're Lucy because you're last. On the list, you put everyone ahead of yourself. Probably at the office, too. But Chai Tea Latte with coconut milk? It's like your only chance to rebel. To show them you don't belong there."

"Where? At my job?"

Cain nods.

"I do too." Lucy's breath quickens. "I work very hard for that company. I streamlined all their systems. Rewrote the handbook and procedures so they actually make sense for employees. The owner relies on me when he's on vacation. That place would fall apart without me."

"Does *that place* appreciate all you do for them? Coming back in for more coffee? I'd have at least gone home to change clothes. Maybe called in sick."

"They're expecting the drinks." Lucy's voice is barely above a whisper. "I can't let them down."

"Why?"

Lucy is late for the staff meeting. Exceedingly late. Without her there to schedule employee evaluations and discuss first quarter projections, she is confident that her coworkers have all devolved into discussing the latest episode of some reality show where everyone yells and throws wine into their supposed friends' faces. Some show Lucy does not watch because it makes her sad. Not knowing for certain, Lucy has assumed friends would be kind to one another. They would bring hot coffees. They would look forward to spending scheduled time together every week and not have to be bribed into showing up.

"What time is it?" Lucy asks Cain, who has spent a considerable amount of time with her this morning, by choice.

"Late," he says.

Lucy nods and blinks back tears. No one has even called her to determine if she is alive and well.

"I've never been late," she says. "Not once in ten years. They aren't my friends, are they?"

"Their loss."

Lucy should smile in response, but she can't do it. She pulls her phone out, not to check the time or to look for nonexistent notifications. She opens the calculator widget and does some quick math, confirming that Cain, the Tattoo Coffee Man, at a standard, minimum wage plus average three hundred dollars in tips per week earns less than she, Office Manager of ten years for a commercial insurance brokerage, does. Barely. It doesn't help her feel proud. Not anymore.

"I gotta go," Cain says with his expected grin. "Back to my job where I make the drinks according to written procedures and exchange standard pleasantries with the customers. My co-workers and I like to chat after the morning rush. If you're ever in search of a job like that, *we* are always in need of reliably hard workers. Especially those who like to streamline systems."

Cain walks to the entrance doors and turns for one last comment.

"You'd get to dress more comfortably, too."

"I like comfortable," Lucy says.

"Tell you what. Make a list of all the pros and cons for leaving your job. Bring it next week at seven fifty-five on the dot, okay?"

Lucy also likes making lists.

She sits in the car for an indeterminate amount of time trying to decide if she will go home and call in sick or continue into the office as is her routine. Nodding, Lucy smiles and shifts the car into reverse. She whispers beeping sounds and pulls out of the parking space. After a safe pause, she flips her signal to the right and moves on.

# STUDIES IN LONGING

*Poem by Eve Müller*

1.

I thought I understood longing. A simple equation—lush wish for the bird that forever escapes the hand's cage.

At twenty-one years, I was heavily into Lacan. Absence a cancer cell lurking within every star and bright blossom, every fold of skin.

A friend gave his little sister a handful of M&Ms, and she began to weep. *Why?* he asked. *Because I know I'm going to eat them,* she cried.

2.

Sex is like that. The end of touch already implied by the first ripple of hand reaching for haunch.

3.

Childhood was nearing its end. Desire burbled up fresh and uncomplicated as a river's headwaters. I lay at the bottom of a heap of sweat-fresh bodies. Cheek crushed against grass. Sensing that somewhere in the pile, Marvin Manning lay, too.

Longing mixed with bruising.

4.

Or the girl who bent to tie my sneaker. Her fingers against my ankle tender as
moths. I can still summon the fluttering.

5.

At the foot of Mt. Vesuvius, archaeologists discovered remains of two women curled together in bed. The couple preserved in a shell of ash, exact shape of their final embrace. But when skin and tissue rotted away, the women left voids.

Is this the essence of longing? Prefiguration of the hollowed-out places that once held tongues, napes, thighs?

# IT ENDS LIKE THIS

*Fiction by Craig Selbrede*

When Saul was twelve, his Irish wolfhound (an aged, spindly creature) stopped eating. Sparky had been peaked for the past few days, and while he was far from the spry puppy he'd once been, Saul felt that the dog should've been aging better. Saul's younger brother, Jonas, had been inconsolable, sobbing uncontrollably as the vet informed them of the diagnosis. Sparky was sick, very sick. And he wasn't going to get better. The best course of action, Dr. Williams, DVM, had said, would be to help him pass quickly and with grace, which disturbed Saul.

Sparky was always more of Jonas' than Saul's...sleeping at the end of the younger boy's bed, following him around the house with loyal enthusiasm, and heeding his calls as if they were terribly, terribly urgent. He'd never seemed to have liked Saul quite as much. Every time Saul told him to sit, he'd stand. If he told him to stay, he'd bolt away. Sparky and Saul were not friends. But nevertheless, he didn't see why Sparky should have to die.

As Sparky's condition worsened, Saul and Jonas' parents sat them down in their neat, sterile, middle class living room—the one they saved for special occasions—and told Saul and Jonas he'd have to be euthanized.

"Why?" Saul asked.

"Because he's not happy anymore," Saul's father had said gently, placing a shaking hand on Saul's shoulder.

"We can't just kill him," Jonas said insistently. "He's family."

"Sometimes you have to love things and let them go," Saul's mother said.

"Not Sparky," Jonas said. "Please. Not Sparky."

"We have to," Saul's father said.

But Jonas was persuasive, younger siblings were like that, and so their parents agreed to give Sparky a little more time. As the days passed, Sparky began to thin in stature and personality, retreating into himself as his body shut down. Jonas begged him and begged him to get better, but Sparky was stubborn in his decay, hollowed out by pain. Soon, Jonas could hardly bear to look at his beloved dog, and it fell to Saul to take care of him.

Saul was sitting in the family room, doing his homework, half his attention trained on precalc and the rest fixated on Sparky's slow, strangled breaths. They bore into Saul's focus, yanking his attention from the numbers until finally he snapped.

"Would you just shut up and die?" He spat at the dog he'd never had the patience for.

For the very first time, Sparky did as Saul said.

When Saul was twenty-five, he sat in Jonas' cluttered dormitory, eyes darting between the crumpled piece of paper in his hand and the trophies lining the walls. Jonas wasn't a star athlete (far from it), but he'd collected a variety of trinkets and trophies from participating in various sports, trinkets he proudly displayed to his friends, roommates, and flings on a plain IKEA bookshelf. Saul wondered what it felt like to value mediocrity. He'd never been good at that. When he graduated from this same university with a chemistry degree, he thought he'd go somewhere. But his grades were just okay, the economy was getting worse every day, and soon enough Saul was back living with his parents, working at a rickety local liquor store alongside fellow burnouts. It was hard, back-breaking, nasty work, and Saul had begun to fantasize about killing himself.

This wasn't new; he'd always felt a tickle of suicide at the back of his neck, ever so slightly, demanding he consider the possibility that he didn't deserve to live. He didn't know when it had started, but it was there when his friends found love in high school while he was getting diagnosed with autism. It was there when he came out as gay and his mother looked at him with that disappointed look she only bothered to half-hide nowadays. Saul had gotten tired of fighting it. Every day got worse, and he was hollow. Saul was ready to die.

And that brought him here, to his brother's dorm, sitting there feeling an aching mix of jealousy and self-hatred that robbed the air from his lungs. Saul tried not to hyperventilate. An anxiety attack right now wouldn't serve his purposes. He just had three trips to make today, and he could move on.

The door swung out and Jonas pushed his way inside, carrying a large stack of textbooks as he prattled excitedly into the phone he held to his shoulder with his head. "Yeah, it's gonna be sick, and…" He sighted Saul. Something like disappointment flashed behind his eyes.

"Give me a sec," he told whoever he was calling. He hung up and turned to his older brother.

"Saul. What are you—?"

"I need something," Saul said concisely. There was no point in dragging this out.

"Well, clearly," Jonas snorted.

Saul reached into his backpack and pulled out the clipboard, with the form attached to it. He had stained it earlier that day, its pure white color flecked with coffee and tears. Jonas looked at it, swallowing.

"They told me you were thinking about it," Jonas said. "But I didn't think you'd really do it."

"I just need your signature, and I'll be gone," Saul said tightly.

"I know how the CARE program works," Jonas shook his head in disbelief. "I've heard about it. You actually went to your doctor, told them you wanted to kill yourself, and he decided to let you?"

"He hasn't let me do anything," Saul pointed out. "Not yet."

"That's right," Jonas scoffed. "Because you need these signatures first. Three of them. Each chosen by that weird-ass A.I. that runs the department. One from a person who loves you…I assume that's me?"

Saul nodded, averting his gaze and staring at an eighth-place swim team ribbon on Jonas' shelf. It was taped up next to a photo of Sparky.

"Right. So one from me, one from a stranger, and one from somebody who's both…whatever that means. You really expect me to let you kill yourself?"

Saul shrugged. "Not really. It'd be nice though."

"God." Jonas was getting hysterical. It was one of those things Saul didn't care for about him. "You're not even going to explain it?"

"What's there to explain?" Saul said. "I want to die."

"Have you even tried to live?"

"What the fuck do you know about what it's like to live like I do, Jonas?" Saul snapped. "I spend every day sitting there, vibrating, hating myself and wishing my meds did more than keep me complacent. I go to work and lug heavy boxes for minimum wage, alongside people who don't give two shits about the job or about me. I come home and our parents scream at me for things I already hate myself for."

For a long moment, Jonas was quiet. Then he shrugged. "Fuck it," he laughed, grabbing a pen and scrawling his name on the contract. "There you go. Are you happy?"

"That's sort of the problem," Saul said impassively. He took the contract and shoved it back into his backpack. The two brothers stared at each other, the distance between them immeasurable.

"I love you," Jonas said, his voice low and broken.

"I know," Saul managed a slight smile. He got to his feet, shrugged the backpack over his shoulder, and patted his brother on the shoulder. "But sometimes you have to love things and let them go."

Saul met the stranger named on his contract in the park a few blocks down Main Street. Saul had always liked this park.

She approached him gingerly, a thirty-something woman with broad-rimmed glasses and the ugliest sweater he'd ever seen. "Hi, uh, hi," she stammered, coming up towards Saul.

"Hi," Saul said, not bothering to meet her eyes.

"I'm Annie," she said. "I don't know you."

"I think that's the point," Saul reminded her.

"Yes, right," Annie swallowed. "And you want me to let you die."

"Yes," Saul said. "Will you?"

Annie hesitated, and Saul sighed. He reached into his backpack, pulling out a wad of cash. His tips for the last two years, meticulously saved for this very purpose. He slid them towards Annie, whose eyes widened.

"Are…are you serious?" She gaped. "You're trying to bribe me?"

"Yes," Saul said. "Is it working?"

"No! No," Annie shook her head. "Jesus, kid. You're…what, 28?"

"25," Saul corrected her.

"Whatever," she shook her head. "You have so much to live for."

"You said it yourself," Saul said. "You don't know me."

"I don't want this on my conscience," Annie shook her head. "This whole system…it's so messed up. Some robot told you that you could die if I said yes?"

Saul was getting impatient. "I can get you more. Money, I mean."

"Do I look like I care about money?"

"You look like you should," Saul said. He was never good at hiding his opinions of people. It was probably why nobody liked him.

Annie took in a shaky breath. "This is messed up," she said, repeating herself. "It's so messed up."

"Life is messed up," Saul said. "I'm done with it."

Annie shrugged. "Well, I, I'm sorry, but I'm not signing that."

Saul sighed.

"Just remind yourself," Saul said. "I wasn't a good person. Not good at living. And not very nice. The world will be no worse off."

"I don't believe that" Annie sputtered.

"What are you, Annie," Saul snickered. "A librarian?"

"I'm…I'm a teacher," Annie said timidly.

"Well, Annie," Saul raised his voice ever so slightly. "Who the fuck are you to keep me trapped in an existence I hate? Why do you get to keep me suffering just because you don't want my death on your conscience? They say you can't stop suicide. But you can make it painless. Tell me, Annie, do you want my death to hurt? You can't keep me alive. But you can make it painless."

Annie stared at Saul for a long, long minute. And then, doubt flickering behind her green eyes, she snatched the contract from him and signed her name.

"This is messed up," she repeated once more.

"Never said it wasn't," Saul shrugged.


Saul stared at the final name on his contract. Quincy Adams. Jonas' best friend through all of middle and high school, until one day they just stopped talking. Saul had half-forgotten he'd ever existed. And now Quincy held Saul's freedom in his hands.

Saul sighed, stood up, and began to pace. He'd have to find a way to reach Quincy, and he'd have to be convincing. He wasn't sure he'd be able to persuade Quincy. He had heard Annie's name around town, but Quincy was an unknown quantity. He'd have to be delicate, and he'd have to be prepared, and—

Ding!

Saul groaned, and, with as much passion as he could muster, marched to the front door. He threw it open, opened his mouth, and froze as he recognized a familiar face. "Quincy?"

"Hey, man," Quincy nodded, his hands shoved into his ratty, thrift-coat pockets. Saul had always hated vintage clothes. They'd gone out of fashion for a reason. "Can I come in?"

Saul closed his mouth and thought for a second.

"Come on, bro," Quincy rolled his eyes. "You want that signature, don't you?"

Well, he had Saul there. Plastering on as legitimate of a smile as he could muster, Saul stepped aside and gestured towards the kitchen. "Please, come in."

"Yeah, sure," Quincy said, pushing past him. Saul hesitated and followed the younger man inside.

"Jonas called me," Quincy sat opposite Saul at the kitchen table, his hard gaze refusing to leave the older man's eyes. "He warned me my name was on the list."

"Right," Saul said. Internally, he swore. He'd been sloppy.

"You know I hadn't heard from him in years?" Quincy said, shaking his head. "Years, man. And then he calls me and tells me I'm the only one who can save his brother."

Saul snorted. "So dramatic."

Quincy's gaze grew sharper, if even possible. "Is it?"

Saul swallowed. He fumbled through his mental reserves, pulling out the prepared speech he'd used on Annie. "You don't know what it's like, Quincy. You have no idea what—"

"Yeah, I don't give a fuck," Quincy cut him off.

Saul blinked.

"If you want to kill yourself, I'm not going to stop you," Quincy said. "I'm also not going to be a party to it."

"What's that supposed to mean?" Saul said. "You can't stop me. But you can make it—"

"Painless, yeah, sure," Quincy said. "Painless for you, maybe."

"What?" Saul sputtered. "Do you have any idea how selfish you sound?"

"Do you have any idea how selfish *you* sound?" Quincy crossed his arms. "If you want to kill yourself, kill yourself. Don't commit suicide by committee."

"You don't know me," Saul said.

"You don't know *me*," Quincy laughed. "Dude, your brother was my best friend for *years*. And I idolized you. Because he idolized you. I loved you. Because he loved you."

"So you're looking out for Jonas?" Saul rolled his eyes. "He already signed the contract. He had his chance."

"It shouldn't be up to him to drag you through life," Quincy said.

"But it's up to you?"

"Again, not stopping you. Just not helping you."

"What the fuck is your problem?"

"My father died, Saul," Quincy said simply.

Saul frowned. "You mean your sucky, deadbeat father?"

"I mean my father," Quincy sneered. "My human, living father who could've changed and found happiness if he'd just tried. I told him to get his act together, and do you know what the fucker did? He went, got three signatures, and killed himself."

"I'm not your father, Quincy," Saul's voice was tight.

"He didn't deserve to die," Quincy murmured. "He wasn't perfect, but he was mine. And now there's a hole in my life that didn't have to be there."

"It is such bullshit that you think I should keep living so others can feel better about themselves."

"And it's such bullshit that you think you should die so you don't have to face yourself." Quincy said. "My man, your life sucks. No shit. Everybody's life sucks."

Saul bit back a sharp comment. He had to salvage this. He could feel his chance at escape slipping away, falling through his fingers like sand in an hourglass. "I don't owe you my life."

"And I don't owe you death," Quincy replied simply. "Kill yourself if you must. But don't rope me into it."

"Just, just think…" Desperation seeped into Saul's voice. "About what you're condemning me to."

"It's not our place to hold each other's lives in our hands," Quincy said. "If you want, I'll save you. But I won't kill you."

"You're such a fucking hypocrite," Saul said. "If you felt what I felt—"

"I never will," Quincy said. "And that's not fair. But that's life."

He got to his feet, clapped Saul on the shoulder, and grabbed his coat. "I hope you choose to live. But if you don't, that's not on me."

The door slammed shut. Saul sat alone in the kitchen.

His gaze darted to the knife block sitting by the fridge. His escape route, so beautifully simple, was gone. And now he had two choices…a painful life or a painful death.

Saul stood up, walked over to the knife block, and drew the biggest, sharpest one. He felt hot, stinging tears well in his eyes, as desperation coursed through him like lightning. Death and Life loomed over him, equally unconcerned with the man caught in between.

The knife clattered to the floor and Saul let out a slow, strangled breath. In the distance, he heard the light pattering of paw steps, as if an old friend was padding away, departing his dreams for both of their sakes.

# LET IN

*Poem by Patrick Reardon*

Let Emmanuel in the door,
like Elijah, like a cold wind, like the
gray mouse seeking warmth, the shoo-fly
in random flight, a random memory, a
gesture offhand, hands over head in
dance, in other circumstances, hands
out to embrace, grab, ward off, a ward
of the state, the state of play, an
open state—

let Emmanuel in,
like a glimmer of something at the edge,
the gasp of something at the end, hate
uncopied, cruelty endured, durable
marble worn by faithful feet, durable
walls around a juvenile city, full of vigor
and vim, boostered like a box of Lux soap
flakes, blind to its own heartbeat—

let in,
like pine scent and needles, like holidays
unfilled, half-finished like a puzzle with
pieces from another box, like a found key,
like a dash of salt in the pot, the weary
shrug of neutrality, those (all of us) sitting
together at the sinners' table, like coming
into focus, like noises ringing true.

Let Jack of Lent in the door,
like a worm but no man, like a bluebottle
on alabaster, thick unto death, like a
nameless voyage to a shallow city, like the
wren of victory, like a stone cracked open
to the unfluid within—

let Jack of Lent in,
like a station of a frivolous cross, like a
coonskin cap odor, like ordure Job-sat,
Job-shat, like sleepless ones, circus
factions, the hall of twenty-three couches, the
heavenly halls, giddy beatitude,
poor-sinner's porch, like a bust of red
porphyry, purple red, hard as the earth's
core and wiser than the Lady Wisdom,
like bright sun beyond the Hamm's sign—

let in,
like light duty, like beam of light, like
bean counting, like the Just One in the
tilted stained-glass in summer heat at
afternoon funeral and, outside, the
endless greens of the tree in sun and
caring shadow, like the undertaken and
the undertaking, the taking of names and
the naming of monsters and rivers and
oysters, like the cut-off ear, like the
Temple servant's question, like the
stigma of barrenness.

Let One-Cent in the door,
like flames of spice, perfumed blaze, fed
by seeds, fruits, roots and barks, herbs
and flavors and garnish, like rope-necked
maids in a row, like the maid burned at the
post for visioning voices, like the woman's
voice singing "Surrey with the Fringe on Top,"
like the black Christmas rose with dark
leathery leaves, like anger at the hole of
breathing, the insufficiency of bald reason,
the wordlessness of agony—

let One-Cent in,
like the alley horse clopping a psalm, like
jade girls with bound feet, like the house
of multitudes, the house of prostitutes, the
International House of Pancakes, like the
joyful precincts of an empty city, the gnat
in the white wine, like private liturgy,
owned scripture, monetized belief, like the
ghetto blizzard, the black bird of morning,
like Abraham, Isaac and Jacob, like Abraham,
Martin and John—

let in,
like the joker rat pioneering through ash,
cinders, soil to the garage floor cement
crack and another route to anywhere, like
unknown words said, like wide panic,
cloistered functions, ruins read, gaps
toted, the sum of all fears, birdsong
translations and bad blood, like a hot gust,
like spirit and dust conversing, like cosmic

grit and every breath a flame and every woe
a joy, like all shall be well, like a cure for
insanity, melancholy, gout and epilepsy, like
anger at the existence of pain, like GirlJane
who wrote "Mad at the World" for the
*Beautiful Desert*
album and Jacoba who
bottled her pain to an ugly vintage.

# FINGER FOODS FOR FAILED APOPTOSIS

*Poem by Pixie Bruner*

They claim cancer eats you alive.
All those cells with razor teeth
rows upon rows, Cuisinarts
macerating microscopic sharks
gnawing the non-cancerous tissue
but cancer doesn't gnaw or eat you.

The pain does,
in small unseasoned bites.
Our bodies are finger foods of
apoptosis' failings.

Cancer doesn't get fuel from sugar,
glucose feeds all cells alike,
all cells can find alternative fuels.
Your body is a broken-down Tesla
on a flat-bed tow truck,
an oh-shit dashboard
*check engine light*
dressed as a human being.

Cancerous growths are unborn monsters.
We call the oncologist and surgeons
to deliver the tumors from us.
We rarely give them names,
pathology and radiation tattoos,
scars are their only marked graves.
Hospice doulas exist to help us cross over
the great chasm from life to not-life.

Metastases are just expansion,
like the lungs expand to let in air,
rogue cells on manifest destiny,
wanting their forty organs and a mule
We make fences they cross
like borders but no one
wants to say "mine" with pride
when new property is claimed by them.

When the diagnosis comes,
the scans and tests confirmed,
there is no congratulation
or gift bag or showers
with humiliating party games
planned by well-meaning friends preparing
for your new family member
that will take over the house.

No one screams "get clean rags
and boil the water!"
no one ever dare says
"Call the midwife for death."

# STITCHES

*Fiction by Jaimee Walls*

Frankie squirmed in bed and listened to the relentless plinking sound of sleet as it mingled with the rhythmic sounds of her heart monitor. She yanked the patches off and unwound herself from the wires that ensnared her. Seattle's winter sky was even more gloomy than usual. It figured that her seventeenth birthday would get rained out. *What kind of plans can a teenager always on the verge of death have anyway?*

When she wasn't busy dying, Frankie liked to read or write. She preferred the dark and gothic: Poe, Stoker, Wilde, and her favorite writer, Shelley. Writing about dying took the mask off of her fear and exposed the pain to hopefulness. Though lately, her body hadn't been giving her much hope.

Climbing out of bed, Frankie lobbed aside a well-worn copy of *Frankenstein* and glowered out the window. Before she could walk, talk, or remember, she'd had her first surgery, a pattern that continued year after year—to the point where she felt like more of a science experiment than a human being. She'd survived different types of heart and brain surgeries, and dozens of other procedures and treatments. But not one decision about her body had ever been her own.

Frankie trudged into the bathroom and stepped into the shower. A migraine was already building as the hot water cascaded over her. She ran her hands through her hair, fingers finding the furrows where hair follicles refused to grow. Lonely tears fell from her eyes.

When she finished and was drying off, Frankie studied her reflection in the mirror. Her hand traced a pink scar that ran from neckline to left breast, which was now almost non-existent. Lines of pink, red, and white left hash marks over her heart. The left breast puckered against these repeated incisions while the right one perked normally. A dark scar split her chest down the middle. The image jarred her, as if she saw the pieces of herself stitched together. The feeling of scars beneath her fingertips stayed with her as she dressed. Frankie pictured the disfigured Frankenstein and the tapestry of scars, which made them both who they were. The scars she bore on the outside were nothing compared to the scars she bore on the inside. They had become a patchwork of guilt—one she could never shake. Though she'd done nothing wrong, pain surged across her skull in pulsing waves.

On instinct, she reached for her migraine medicine. Despite the warnings from her doctors, she'd quit taking all prescriptions days ago. Now, the dozen bottles stared at her from the countertop. Even with a migraine barreling down on her like a freight train, the last thing she wanted to do was take a pill.

She grabbed the trash can and picked up the closest bottle. Seeing a string of letters she could barely pronounce, unable to recall why she took it, she tossed it in the can. The next one was to prevent seizures. She hesitated but tossed it in the can too.

"Won't be needing you anymore." She tossed it.

The next was to regulate her hormones. Frankie squinted at the bottle. She hated being told how to feel.

"Whatever!" In the can.

She picked up a medication supposed to prevent migraines. In the can.

This rant continued until she held the final bottle. It was for her heart. Even though it was the same size as the others, it felt weighty. Frankie shook it and listened as the pills rattled inside. Taking a steadying breath, she tossed it angrily into the can. It pinged and clanged on its way to the bottom.

Holding the trash, she sighed.

*No more doctors cutting her open.*

*No more surgeries digging into her heart.*

*No more medications messing with her body.*

No matter what happened next, things would be as nature intended. Even if it was a death sentence. The thought of telling her parents about this decision made her nauseous. They'd lived with her dying every day.

Her death would be like watching a house they built burn to the ground. *Was her choice so selfish?*

*A better daughter would do what her parents told her.*

*A better daughter would do what the doctors said.*

*A better daughter would fight harder to live.*

After all, they only wanted what was best for her. Frankie had witnessed how her illnesses bankrupt her parents. *Hadn't they fought hard enough? Done enough? Hadn't she?*

"Francesca?" Mom knocked on the door. "Are you coming to breakfast?"

She sighed, choking back tears then swallowed hard before answering. "In a minute, Mom."

Frankie steeled herself; from the hallway she watched her parents in the tiny kitchen. The overwhelming scent of applewood bacon drifted to her. Dad leaned over the stove, stirring eggs into the bacon grease while Mom squeezed in beside him, putting candles onto a chocolate cake. Their elbows grazed past each other as they worked side by side. It was a rare sight to see them together like this.

Long gone were the morning sunrises over the lake and the mountain sunsets. The drives to the hospital took minutes now instead of hours. Yet every year, her world got smaller. Frankie glanced at the small end table where Mom managed the household finances. A stack of unpaid bills had morphed into an untamed beast even with Dad's two jobs.

"Happy Birthday!" Mom and Dad said in unison. Mom held out the small cake with homemade whipped frosting. "Make a wish," Mom whispered. Her eyes sparkled in the candlelight.

Frankie wished science wouldn't stitch her together ever again. Her wish was to die with some grace and dignity, at home, in her own bed. Her wish wasn't selfish. She wasn't really choosing death. It had chosen her a long time ago.

She blew out the candles.

"Mom, Dad," her voice shook, "I'm not taking any more medications."

Her parents stared at each other and then at her.

"I haven't *been* taking them." With each word she spoke, she felt lighter.

"But…"

"I'm done with my appointments and surgeries too. All of it. I'm done."

The truth was out. Frankie watched the tears fall from Mom's eyes—a slow leak—drip, drip, drip. Mom wiped them away with boney hands. *When had her mom's hands gotten so small, so thin, so frail?* Pain spasmed Frankie's heart as she watched her parents' crumble.

"Why?" asked Mom. Frankie studied the lines on her mother's face. The years were showing, every stitch, every sleepless night, every fear.

"Keeping me alive like this has never been my choice, Mom. It's yours. It's Dad's." She threw up her hands. "It's modern medicine's." She allowed all the feelings swirling through her to rush to the surface. "I'm angry and I'm scared. I could see a point to it if I were getting better," she paused. "But I'm not getting better. I'm done." She let her head sag. "And I'm just so tired."

"This is a big decision. We need to talk to your doctor about this first," Dad said.

"No, Dad. *We* don't need to do anything!" she shouted. Searing pain tugged unevenly at her heart. "I just want to be left alone." Frankie begged. She tromped down the hall to her room and slammed the door behind her. Why wouldn't anyone just listen to her? It was as though she was a ragdoll. They did whatever they wanted to with her. She stared at her shaking hands.

She felt wracked with pain and guilt; her stomach fretted for the food she should've eaten. All that amazing cooking on the other side of the door and she'd stormed out. She couldn't go back and grovel now. The thought of eating didn't feel good anyway. Tears she'd held back fell past her lashes.

"Oh, for fuck's sake." Frankie wrapped her head between her arms and rocked herself. Even with all she'd been through, the Universe would take her out of this world kicking and screaming. She'd get no peace, no justice, no relief.

She managed to get back to the bathroom and dug the migraine medicine out of the trash. After fighting with the packaging, she broke a pill free and washed it down with water from the sink. Depleted, she climbed into bed, curling into a ball under a cloud of blankets, and cried.

Frankie woke to total darkness. Fear gripped her. Moments passed before it dawned on her that she had slept through the day. Her throbbing pulse whooshed through her head and ears as if she were under the rotor blades of a helicopter. Pain stabbed like needles through skin.

Once Frankie's eyes adjusted, she fumbled with the nightstand light. Sighing, she settled into the pain and propped herself up with pillows so she could write. The scents of wood and lead filled her nose as the pencil scratched its way across a blank page. Words tangled and twisted with fears and frustrations as the white space faded. Dark saucy twists animated things that should be dead while she tried to grasp why she still lived.

She wrote for a while and penned this poem:

*Bones live forever but flesh is a feast.*
*Sickness feeds on life and swallows the unleashed.*
*A path to death is anchored to dreams.*
*Life leads us on until somebody screams.*
*Stitched together like sounds on a track,*
*Life finds a way and then never comes back.*
*Leafless trees hang in indigo skies,*
*Mists and darkness always tell lies.*

A knock on the door surprised her. "Fran…Frankie?" Opening the door a sliver, Mom poked her head through, her eyes red and swollen. "Can we come in?"

Frankie forced herself to sit up straighter. "Sure." She set the notebook and pencil aside.

They came in with a present, a piece of birthday cake, and a glass of water. Dad set them on the nightstand and arranged them in a nervous and methodical order, switching places until they were right.

"We're sorry." Mom reached out and took Frankie's hand. "You're right. This is your decision. We canceled your appointments with the doctor." Mom sniffled. "Is there anything you need?"

Frankie shook her head.

"Let us know if you change your mind. We can get someone to come care for you, manage the pain…" said her father.

"No." Tears welled in her eyes, but she kept them from falling. "You've done enough, Dad." Frankie tried to smile.

"It's obvious how much pain you're in." Mom squeezed her hand. "What if it gets worse?"

"We spoke with a care manager who could come by tomorrow and do an evaluation." Dad swallowed and cleared his throat. "See where you are…in the process." He wiped his eyes and looked away.

"Or we could have…" Mom trailed off as Frankie shook her head. Mom swallowed the lump in her throat and handed her the package. "Go on then, open your birthday present," she said, her voice pitched high.

Frankie struggled to unwrap it. Her arms were weak and heavy. A leather-bound journal—her hand traced over the engraved cover etched with the tree of life, the roots diverging out as far as the branches themselves. When she opened it, the spine cracked, and the scent of fresh paper wafted up to her nose, relaxing her.

"It's beautiful, Mom. Thank you."

"You write in all those creative ideas of yours." Mom's eyes glistened with tears.

Frankie held the journal close to her chest and nodded. They both kissed her on the forehead, kisses full of grief and forgiveness.

"Rest, honey. We love you," said Mom.

"I love you both too."

After they closed the door behind them, she couldn't write. She didn't touch the cake, or the water either. Instead, she picked up her well-worn copy of *Frankenstein* and began to read. Frankie once again found comfort by relating to Frankenstein—both were alive but wouldn't be without science.

Like Frankenstein, she found herself friendless, with no one to talk to or who understood. They both had their physical deformities, stitched together like macabre dolls. He was angry like her too. Both were frustrated by a world that didn't understand them. Couldn't. Defective casualties of science and brutal aspirations. Tears slid past her lids as she closed them.

Frankie let the book fall to her chest. The beats of her heart slowed to a murmur. Pain faded. Regrets floated past her, never having kissed anyone or fallen in love, never graduating from school or going to college, never visiting a spooky ancient castle in Wales, never becoming a published author, and never knowing what other possibilities could've been…

Behind her closed eyes, the light around her transformed into something mystical and surreal. Trees branched out, and brilliant leaves fluttered around her. She stretched out her arms as far as they would go. The vision enchanted Frankie, lifting her into it, like words weaving a story on a page. All her anger quelled as if a storm had passed and, in the hush, she heard the plinking sounds of strings—it almost sounded like the *Happy Birthday* song.

# THE BALLAD OF YOUNG MRS. FRANKENSTEIN

*Visual Art by Kat Tabor*

# ENOUGH

*Poem by Anne Marie Fowler*

I thought I'd seen enough of the winter here at the base
of the Rockies, specifically the Northern tier of the Springs

where the raspy chatter of the magpie settles between the white pine's
branches, its young not yet ready to teeter on goodbye.

Pike's Peak is still frosted over when the heat threatens to melt it;
the hail comes anyway, tinks and bounces off the top of the grill,

thuds on the peeling deck where it collects like a carpet. The stucco
on the north wall of the house still reels from last year's storm.

Tonight, I listen to the drum of rare rain after the hail and recall
nights in the Midwest where rolling thunder was comfort, the lightning

a beautiful sky show, the air outside blissfully green grass and clean linen.
Through the bay window a hush falls heavy, the hail ending, sun
     beginning.

I see the neighbor's cat in its window, think of the mountain lion tucked
among the rocks, its breath hot against the fallen snow, paw prints
     hidden

from the hunter who will still surely find them at the crack of dawn
when the lion's hunger drives it out to hunt, it, too, having had enough
     of winter's storm.

# FRITZ THE GROCERY MAN

*Fiction by Joe Michael Feist*

"That's tree turdy-tree."

"How much?" the kid giggled.

"Tree dollars and turdy-tree cents."

The boy, ten or twelve, laughed like a clown with a frog in his pants. Fritz Kaufmann looked down at the counter again. A loaf of bread, a pound of onions and two packs of bubble gum. "*Ja.* Tree turdy-tree."

Fritz had a wicked German accent. The kid liked to hear him say turdy. Turdy-tree was even funnier. That's why he got the bubble gum, carefully calculated to push the total up to tree turdy-tree. A lot of boys came into the Mesto Grocery Store to buy groceries for mama. They all liked to hear Fritz say turdy. Fritz knew the game but paid no mind. He thought it was good for their arithmetic.

As the kid scurried away, the corners of Fritz's mouth moved maybe a quarter of an inch. That was his best smile. It was hard for Fritz to be nice and smiley, excruciating. He had the capacity to smile but ignored it—thought it was for the delicate, sentimental types. He was a stout and robust German. It wasn't as if he were angry; the pouty was just glued on.

The Mesto Grocery Store was a staple in Mesto, a tiny Czech and German farming community in hot West Texas. The hamlet was born around 1900 when immigrant farmers looking for good dirt found it.

Fritz loved his old store, though he wondered how long he could keep it. He was pushing eighty now and still feisty, but Mesto was wasting away.

In an uncharacteristic attempt to draw attention to itself and perhaps attract customers from the surrounding towns, the Czech Lodge was sponsoring the "Best Business in Mesto" contest. Its members thought it might be a chance to teach outsiders, again, how to pronounce the name of the town. It wasn't *mess*-toe. It was mee-*es*-toh, the Czech word for "small town." The small town was named small town. It made perfect sense to anyone who lived around the small town of Mesto.

Fritz longed to win the Best Business contest, to be lifted up as an exemplar of Germanic hard work and persistence, business acumen and, yes, good looks. He thought his face was a little narrow for a German, but his blue eyes made up for it. His bald head made him look distinguished. His grocer's apron, he knew, did a commendable job hiding his fair-sized belly.

He needed to win the contest, for his small operation wasn't exactly Piggly Wiggly.

Fritz wanted a soft drink. The sign on his big cooler advertised Coca-Cola, but Fritz kept only a few on hand. He did keep it well stocked with Dr Pepper, a drink he and all decent people preferred.

Then his eyes fixed on a can of Spam, which carried his thoughts back sixty years to Vietnam rations. He was young then but was dubbed Papa Fritz for his good-natured but very German sourness. Because he had good eyesight, the Army, in its infinite wisdom, placed him in reconnaissance. *Ja!* That's the first step, he thought, and he was thrilled.

Mesto had but a handful of businesses, maybe twenty. Elmer Urbanek's Mesto Lumber Yard, catty-cornered from Fritz' grocery store, was a place to start. Fritz and Elmer chatted only a few seconds about the skimpy last rain and Dotty Hoffman dragging Floyd out of Janecek's Bar by the ear. Then Fritz casually brought up the contest. Elmer was going to give away one six penny nail to everyone who came by on judgment day.

Over at Janecek's Bar, Wally Janacek said the contest was stupid and to hell with it. Rudy Hovorak, who owned the Mesto Café and was enjoying a cold one over by the jukebox, said he was too busy trying to make a living for such foolishness.

Fritz strolled down the street to the Mesto Filling Station, which also closed at noon on Saturdays. But usually, Skeeter Vanicek, the owner, and Beto Fuentes, Skeeter's longtime "assistant manager," hung around a while to chit chat and clean up the place. And then there was that new kid, Jimmy Shaughnessy.

Jimmy was sweeping around the pumps. He stopped and smiled when he saw Fritz approaching.

"Afternoon there, Fritz," Jimmy called out.

"*Ja*, how are you, Jimmy? I should've brought you a Dr Pepper."

Skeeter had that grin, like he knew what Fritz was after. "Well, Fritz, since I pushed the idea at the Czech Lodge, I'm looking forward to it. What do you think of the whole thing? Are you joining in?"

"*Ja*, sure," Fritz said, "but what are you doing for the contest? To get votes?"

"Nothin' much," Skeeter said, grinning. There was nothing for Fritz to learn.

At the end of the day's recon mission, Fritz was a mostly satisfied German. The odds were shifting in his favor as businesses dropped out or the owners traveled to *dummkopf* land.

* * *

The next day, after church at Saints Cyril and Methodius, Fritz walked the short path to the tidy cemetery, just as he did every Sunday, and stopped at Angie's grave. It had been seven years since he lost her. He looked straight up.

*Angie? Are you busy, Angie? Listen, I want to win the contest. If He happens to walk by or something, can you put in a good word for me? Tell Him I cleared some space next to the toothpaste for votive candles and saints' medals. And I'll only charge wholesale. Maybe slightly more.* Auf wiedersehen, *Angie.*

Fritz turned and saw the widow Scrabanek behind Charlie's tombstone by a blooming Texas sage. Albina was a nice first name. She owned and operated the Mesto Beauty Shop. For a reason he didn't understand, he walked toward her, intending to be as nice as possible. He straightened up as best he could, but then vaguely remembered Albina didn't like Germans.

"*Guten Tag*," Fritz said.

"*Dobry den*," she countered in Czech.

He was never good at pleasantries, especially with women. "So, it's a good day, Albina, and do you like Germans?"

Albina looked bewildered. "Some. Who do you like?"

He looked sideways, then up, then sideways again. "Well…I think, maybe, I like, uh…"

Albina was halfway to her car.

* * *

That Monday, Albina appeared in the grocery doorway.

"Good morning, Fritz."

Albina had smooth skin and carried a few extra pounds, which to Fritz only meant she was healthy. He tried to remember her age but couldn't. Anyway, it was close enough to his own, and she still had dark hair and fair features. Of course, she owned a beauty shop so her hair could be any color and….

"Fritz? Fritz? I need a ten-pound bag of flour."

"*Ja*, Albina, I will get it for you."

He placed the flour on the counter. She spoke. "Fritz, I want to ask you, if you don't mind telling me, what are you going to do for the contest?"

I think now she's playing my game, Fritz thought. "I don't know yet. I have so many ideas to choose from. And you, Albina, what do you think about the contest? What are you going to do?"

Albina said she was thinking of showing off her kolaches, maybe giving samples and inviting people to look at her beauty shop to get votes. Albina was well known for her kolaches with buttery sweet dough and delicious fillings. "*Ja*," Fritz said. "Your poppy seed kolache is the best."

Albina thanked him, but then said sadly that she might withdraw due to Rudy Hovorak's brilliant idea for his café. Fritz was confused. "What are you saying? Rudy himself told me he was too busy for a foolish contest."

"Oh, no. Tereza came in last week for a cut and a perm and said that if he won Best Business, Rudy was going to give away a Coca-Cola to anyone who buys a burger on a Wednesday. For a whole year!"

Now Fritz was riled. "Only Coca-Cola? Why not Dr Pepper? Either way, scheisse," he said, then quickly apologized for the profanity. "I never trusted that Rudy. I think he puts breadcrumbs in his hamburger meat, so it looks big. The rascal. Now he's saying he's not playing the game when he is. He can win, even without Dr Pepper. Scheisse!"

Surprising himself, Fritz motioned toward the bench outside the front door. "Why don't we sit, Albina. Tell me something. Do you like what you do?"

It was a hard question for Albina, and she pondered. "To tell the truth, Fritz, it's not fun anymore. It hasn't been since Charlie passed. I'm not happy and my customers can see it. All day I dream about making kolaches. Such a crazy thing, I forget what I'm doing. The other day I was thinking about cottage cheese kolaches, and I dyed Mrs. Holik's hair bright red instead of auburn. Fritz, she looked just like Lucy. And oh, she had a hissy fit."

Fritz let loose a guffaw. He had heard other people guffaw, of course, but to have his first guffaw at his age, well, he was shocked. But he quickly put his German pouty face back on when he sensed her pain.

"I'd rather be making kolache than teasing Gladys Muller's oily hair," Albina said. "Poppy seed. Like you like." She looked up at Fritz when she said poppy seed and smiled like a woman does—in a way he only vaguely remembered.

Then it hit him like a shot of schnapps. The brain under his bald head was working after all. "Albina, you know the storeroom here in my grocery with the big window facing the street. Why don't you close your beauty shop and forget hair. Come make kolaches all day long, next to me. So when people come for an onion, they leave with an onion and kolaches. You keep your money, and I keep mine. Or maybe another arrangement we can make. Sound good?"

Albina looked flabbergasted. "I don't know what to say, Fritz. Are you serious? It's so much to think about. I mean—"

Fritz interrupted. "That's the problem with the world, Albina. Everybody thinks too much. How do you *feel* about it?"

She shook her head to clear the cobwebs. "Yes, Fritz, yes. I *feel* like doing it. But it's crazy."

Her hand brushed his and he wondered if it was an accident. Fritz scratched his bald head. "*Ja,* it's really crazy. But can you see it, Albina, the Mesto Grocery and Kolache Store. And we'll win the contest with your kolaches."

They spent all afternoon at the grocery store, their minds churning with questions and ideas.

He painted a poster, "Closed for expansion," and taped it on the door above the Mrs. Baird's Bread sign. Another went up on the picture window: *Kolaches! Coming soon!* For the next two weeks, Albina and Fritz slaved to make their dream breathe. People began to talk and stop by to watch the work. Since it hadn't rained for a while, there wasn't much else to talk about in Mesto.

On the Monday before the contest judging, Vince Dusek from the Mesto Hardware Store filed a protest with the judges, respected city leaders from over in Markton, the county seat eight miles up the road from Mesto. Vince said the new Mesto Grocery and Kolache Store was two entities, not one, and would have an unfair advantage over other businesses.

"Vince always makes trouble," Fritz fumed. "His papa was the same. Once he put some caraway seeds in a batch of homebrew just to see what it would do. All the men got crazy and started crawling on the roof, howling and fighting their shadows."

Then Fritz changed subjects. "And now the judges. All from Markton."

"Why does that matter?" Albina said calmly.

"Well, when a Marktonite wanders into the grocery, first of all, he's lost. Then he calls me Mr. *Cough-Man,* like I have the whooping cough. I will say, very nice, *nein.* It's *Kowf*-mun. Okay, Mr. *Cough-Man,* they say again. *Dummkopfs!*"

The next day, the judges rejected Vince Dusek's protest, mostly because they, too, had heard of Albina's kolache and wanted to partake.

* * *

On judging day, Fritz and Albina had kolache samples to attract voters. The cottage cheese and apricot were the most popular, but Fritz dismissed the fact. "The good and decent people like poppy seed," he explained to Albina.

With all the commotion of getting the kolache business up and running, Fritz had never come up with any promotion for his grocery store. He did put out some sort-of-fresh apples. Everyone took a kolache, looked at the apples and walked away, or asked for another kolache. Fritz hid his gruff sourness and flashed his quarter-inch smile, which still pained him. By day's end, *ach du lieber* had become Fritz' favorite expression, after *scheisse*. But he was happy for Albina. She was where she wanted to be.

Almost as soon as Albina opened the kolache part of the business, she could barely keep up with sales. Her hands were sore from kneading and mixing, and the big oven was blistering. Fritz came by when he wasn't busy with groceries to accidentally brush against her hand and stir the apricots. The business got so hectic that Albina hired Elmer Urbanek's daughter to help out. And when the people from Markton started buying kolaches and filling his grocery store, Fritz didn't say *Dummkopf* quite as often, unless they called him Mr. *Cough-Man* more than once.

Around six o'clock every day, Fritz and Albina would stop working and sit on the bench outside if it wasn't too hot or go in and sit beside the Coca-Cola cooler so Fritz could easily grab a Dr Pepper.

"Why do you like Dr Pepper so much, Fritz?" Albina asked one day.

"There's just a pop when you swallow," he said. "Like some wines. A peppery taste at the end."

"You know so much, Fritz," she said, smiling. He tried hard to smile back.

"Besides," he added, "I heard it has prune juice in it."

"Ah, then I should try it. And the onions you love?"

"I ate them when I was a baby," he said. That was enough of an explanation.

They talked about their parents and siblings, their first marriages, their moments of joy and loss. They both had three children who had all moved from Mesto. They longed to see more of them and their grandkids, and it was never enough, they agreed.

Fritz looked at Albina one day. "Sometimes I wish I were thirty again. But today, sitting here, I'm very happy to be…older," Fritz said, shocking them both with words totally out of character.

Their chairs beside the Coca-Cola began to inch closer every day.

One afternoon, Skeeter dropped by for a kolache and took Fritz aside. "It looks like you and Albina are really getting along."

"*Ja,*" Fritz said, "business is good."

"I was thinking of something else. You don't have a clue about what's happening between the two of you, do you?"

"What are you saying, Skeeter?"

"Y'all are a couple. Everybody knows it but you."

"I'll think about it," Fritz said.

* * *

One cool day with rain clouds above, Fritz took Albina's floured hands in his. "We should walk to the café," he said. "It's Wednesday. I feel like a hamburger and a free Coca-Cola, if I can't have Dr Pepper. And I have something to ask you."

THE END

# GOODBYE, SALAD

*Poem by Brian Rohr*

Savory seeds,
crunchy kraut,
luminous leaves
flavored with oil,
spicy and rich,
a hint of the earth we tend.

Tossing, flying,
mixed with a perfection that allows for flare.
Colored with carrots, peppers,
even raisins to surprise and pop.

Take time to lap up.
Crunch your way and taste.
Really taste. No need to be too proud.
The earth needs you now in this moment
to understand what can be lost.

Bring the plate to your mouth,
tongue ready to finalize the meal.
Wallow in the last flavor,
herbs and salt, marinated.
So vital, alive.

When the abundance offers itself
so readily, it is hard to remember
our mother is whispering her
final farewell.

# ANGEL WINGS

*Fiction by Sue Pace*

When my little brother, Ryan, was in first grade, he had me run my hands over his back so I could feel the wings growing there. "When I die," he said, "those wings will spring out and I will become an angel. That's what one of the nurses told me." Ryan spent a lot of time in the children's hospital taking various treatments for cancer. On the way home from the hospital, I sat in the back seat with him. I stretched and wiggled, trying to touch my own set of wings.

Two years after Ryan died, I was still struggling to touch my own set of wings. Occasionally, I could see them when I wore my swimsuit and peered over my shoulder at my image in the hazy locker room mirror.

That fall, I asked my teacher, "Are people supposed to grow wings?"

She smiled and said, "Why would you ask that?"

When I told her what my little brother had whispered, she said she wasn't sure how an angel grew wings or whether they even had halos or harps. Then the school bell rang, and she told the class it was time to go home.

Mrs. Duncan's husband taught high-school science, and she brought his plastic skeleton into her classroom after spring break. She instructed us to count each of the two-hundred and six bones. "No wings," she said, "Those flat bones at the back are scapulae but people who aren't medically trained call them shoulder blades."

After class, I stood in front of her desk. "My brother said a nurse told him those were wings. They were going to help him fly into heaven. Was the nurse lying?"

Mrs. Duncan smiled and touched my cheek. That was all.

Months later, my mother died, and my father left me with the aunt-from-hell. After spending a day locked in a closet, I ran away to Mrs. Duncan's and she took me under her wing. That's what she said to the social worker, "My husband and I will take her under our wings."

When I was in eighth grade, the English teacher gave an assignment that was supposed to teach us about different forms of research. I didn't want to research helicopters or airplanes or heading for the moon in a spaceship, but my teacher didn't want a paper about damselflies or geese or the monarch butterflies who travel twenty-five hundred miles.

He only wanted the history of planes and helicopters and rockets. So, I finally wrote a paper about the very first manned flight by the Wright Brothers on December 17, 1903. The Kitty Hawk flight covered the distance of one-hundred and eighty feet in twelve seconds. It was, I wrote, simply a non-tethered frame using the wind and a sandy reef to float over a non-populated beach with a human hanging on and hoping to not crash and die.

My teacher gave me an F for research and an A for perfect spelling, punctuation and accurately presented references. Those letters were combined into a grade of C-. I had never gotten a score so low and never would again. Sometimes anger can be a great motivator. My below average C- did not hold me back but propelled me to the position of Valedictorian of my high school and I ended up with a four-year scholarship at an out of state college.

I never returned to my hometown because Mr. and Mrs. Duncan retired to Cancun, Mexico. They sent me lovely postcards, but it was clear that my future was up to me. I put my head down and plodded forward to complete a degree in social work.

My final counseling internship was at Seattle Children's Hospital. I understood the pain the young patients were going through as well as the agony of parents and siblings as they watched their loved ones sink into a kind of confusion and finally die. I didn't understand the lack of empathy by many of the medical interns but one of the nurses tried to explain to me how unremitting studying and nights without sleep can bring the exhausted students to a stumbling kind of existence.

"Then the university needs to change their training demands," I snapped. She nodded and shrugged and went to check the oxygen levels on the newborns and toddlers.

She is going to the hospital's hospice wing, I thought. It contained a long hallway of isolated rooms for children of all ages to become nothing or to become angels. That's when I understood the need for my brother's nurse, all those years ago, to try to make his descent into oblivion bearable.

It was weeks later, just before the holidays when one of my patients, a little girl, asked me about angels and halos and wings, I replied, "sometimes an idea can be more than one thing."

"My mama said I was going to die but if I prayed real hard, I might get to heaven."

I wasn't a practicing Christian, but I understood the need for a future beyond death. Across the world, all manner of religions had a focus on an ending that was an invisible future. Those religions focused on rebirth, renewal, or residing on clouds of glory. For the evil ones, there was forever burning in a lonesome hell, or eternal submersion at the edge of nothingness.

If I was forced to live for eternity, my hope was that I would simply live in a purgatory that allowed me to plant a garden and share the fruits of my labor.

I stroked the forehead of the young girl and sang songs about playmates and sunshine on our shoulders. The shoulders that held the promise of wings and the delight of dipping and soaring in a sky forever blue.

I watched as the young girl flew away into nothingness. Then I wiped my tears and loosened my shirt so that my own wings could lift me through the doorway and silently glide me to another room at the end of the hallway.

# THE HOUSE THAT WASN'T MEANT TO LAST

*Poem by walker watson*

I built a home in the hollow of your chest,
Fingers raw, weaving warmth into the cracks,
Each brick a truth, each nail a promise—
I thought love was meant to feel like that.

I carved my name into your walls,
Hung my secrets in the halls,
Lit the darkness with your laughter,
Dreamed we'd live here ever after.

But the nights grew cold, the timber bent,
The roof sighed under words unmeant,
I heard your silence in the creaking floors,
Like a ghost that knows it's not wanted anymore.

Then the fire came—slow, merciless, cruel,
It didn't rage, it didn't roar;
It whispered like doubt, like a lover's lie,
And consumed us from the inside.

I watched it climb, that quiet flame,
Turned every tender touch to blame,
It fed on memories we swore were real,
And left me numb, too hurt to feel.

I reached for you through the smoke and haze,
But your hands were embers, your eyes ablaze,
And the house I'd built inside your skin
Collapsed, as if it had never been.

Now I'm left with the charred remains,
A grave of hope, a heart in chains,
Sifting through ashes that once felt warm,
Finding pieces of you in the ruins of the storm.

How cruel, to make a home of trust,
To think love could be built from dust,
Only to find when the flames have passed,
It was never a house that was meant to last.

# HOW TO BE THE ELDEST DAUGHTER

*Fiction by KR Woodruff*

These are the things you do when your father calls to tell you he has cancer.

Sit for a moment in shock. Say to your husband, "Carl, I need some air." Pick up your jacket because you're suddenly freezing, even though it's midsummer and the meteorologist on TV this morning wore a humorless smile when he announced the temperature. Go to the corner store and buy a six-pack of your least favorite beer, so you have a tangible target for your anger. Put four cans in the fridge, give the fifth to Carl, and break your best fingernail opening your own because what the hell, as long as you're having a miserable night anyway, the world might as well add one more insult. Call your sister Amy even though you know she's out with that one woman whose name you always forget. Listen to her go quiet, and when she asks if you need her to come over, tell her no, enjoy your date, we'll talk tomorrow. Hang up and drink your shitty beer at the kitchen table. When Carl asks if you're calling Adrian, tell him to shut the fuck up, you're perfectly capable of contacting your own goddamn siblings and doesn't he know that it's midnight in New York? Immediately feel awful and say you're sorry, it's just a lot, you didn't mean to yell, and you'll call your brother in the morning. Receive your husband's instant forgiveness and wonder for the millionth time how someone like you managed to marry such a kind, beautiful man. Go to sleep in his arms and try to remember if you ever heard your father apologize to your mother. Decide that no, he never did.

These are the things you do the next day.

Call your brother and try not to resent him for sobbing as hard as he does, because it's not his fault he was born the golden son. Pick Amy up so the two of you can drive to the house together, because she's your little sister and it's easier to take responsibility for your family's shortcomings when you tell yourself you're doing it for her, not because it's expected of you and when no one else steps up, you will be the one accused. Sit with her on that peeling faux-leather couch you hate in a dank living room that reeks of cigarettes and dirty underwear. Shout questions at your father over the too-loud TV and get cussed at for shouting. Back in the car, call his doctor, who might be the only person your father resents more than you. Put him on speakerphone and ask him the questions your father refused to hear. Thank the doctor for his time and his condolences. Sit in the car with Amy, the two of you smelling like the worst parts of your childhood. Look into her wide, trusting face and bracingly tell her you'll figure it out. Feel like you did when you were twelve and she was six, hiding from your awful grandmother in the funeral home coat closet, when you promised her that even though your mother was dead, everything was going to be fine, she'd see.

These are the things you do in the days that follow.

Try to have a frank discussion with your father about his care needs. Be told you're not his goddamn mother. Steal the sticky note from his computer monitor that has all his passwords. Spend hours online trying to find what treatment the VA covers and what it doesn't. Ask him for his VA paperwork. Get accused of trying to rob him. Grit your teeth. Call Adrian and tell him to talk to his fucking father, because you're not getting anywhere and if he's going to listen to anyone, he'll listen to his treasured son. Pick Adrian up from the airport the following week and hold him as he weeps in the baggage claim. Sit on your living room floor with Carl, Adrian, Amy, and three moving boxes full of loose papers that your father deigned to release into Adrian's custody. Spend six hours sorting through the financial chaos. Put someone with a thick Indian accent on speakerphone and watch in awe as your fretful little brother becomes charming and confident as he negotiates a labyrinthine bureaucracy. Realize how badly you miss Adrian when he's not around.

These are the people you get to know.

Your father's primary care doctor. Your father's oncologist. Your father's case manager. The green-haired teenagers serving burnt coffee in the hospital cafeteria. The imaging tech who wears a bow tie. The other, far less dapper imaging tech. Ava, the oncology nurse. Brady, the oncology nurse. Maria, the oncology nurse. Three overwhelmed residents on their first rotation. Otto, *the ugly mutt who is contaminating the hospital, he'll take a shit in the hallways, Jesus fucking Christ, this is what happens when you idiots elect a Democrat.* Arnold, Otto's handler, who you take aside on the way out and assure that Otto is a gorgeous therapy dog utterly undeserving of your father's vitriol. Elena, who is your age and has the same chemo schedule as your father. Babs, who takes Elena's spot three weeks later and with a trembling lip explains that she knew Elena from the support group, and she's so sorry to be the one to tell you. Arliss, who comes to talk with your father about joining the cancer support group. George, who comes to talk with your father about joining the veterans' cancer support group. Amanda, the at-home care coordinator. Jose, the security guard who comes to escort your father from the premises the day he starts berating the other chemo patients for being lazy goddamn hippies when someone mentions medical marijuana.

These are the people you never meet.

The driver of the blue Toyota who you see turning into the hospital parking lot so often that you eventually both give a little wave as you pass at the intersection. The third-graders who make every patient a Christmas card. The janitor who fishes your father's Christmas card from the trash and hangs it up in the utility room because its adorable Santa Claus looks a little like Mr. Clean. The person who took your favorite water bottle to the clinic lost-and-found; the person who vacates the cafeteria table in front of the windows when they see you in line with your limp chicken sandwich and decide you look like you need the sunshine more than they do.

This is how you feel.

Exhausted. Frustrated with your asshole father and his continued obstinacy; scared, because this is all uncharted territory. Embarrassed, because he is rude and disrespectful to the people trying to keep him alive. Angry that you have to deal with his shit. Overwhelmed, because you're in charge and you have no idea what you're doing. Nauseous, because in the deepest, darkest, most awful part of your black little heart, no matter how miserable you are, you're still getting the sick satisfaction of watching your father die in pain.

These are the emblems of his vanishing dignity.

A scabby, chemo-bald scalp. The nasal cannula from his oxygen concentrator. A walker with fresh neon tennis balls on its feet. The huge blue veins that pop out as he struggles to get himself from the bed to his recliner. Diego, the home health aide who ignores being called a filthy Mexican while your father sits naked and bony on a shower chair and afterward tells you that it mostly doesn't bother him because he's from El Salvador, not Mexico, and in any case, he's not the one needing a bath. Urinal bottles hanging from the edge of your father's bed when the cancer metastasizes into his spine; adult diapers, when he stops being able to use the bottles. Powdered food thickener you mix into his applesauce when he stops being able to swallow liquids. Little sponge-sticks like tiny toilet brushes to moisten his lips when he stops being able to swallow at all.

This is what your father says to you the day he dies.

*I want Adrian. Get Adrian in here.*

This is what you say back.

*He's on a plane. He's on his way.*

This is the last thing your father says to anyone.

*So goddamn useless.*

These are the things you do after the body is taken away.

Tell Adrian that if he wants a funeral, he can plan it his own fucking self. Feel chagrined when he pulls out his credit card and pays for a subdued, classy afternoon that your father doesn't deserve at all. Listen to his heartfelt speech about the ways your father somehow managed to not fail as a father. Listen to your sister's own gentle eulogy, in which she thanks you for your role in his last days. Hear one of your distant cousins mutter, "Not even for her own father. How selfish," when you yourself decline to eulogize the person you hate most in this world.

Briefly consider flushing the ashes down the toilet. Get handed a cold-cut sandwich and almost cry when you bite into a pickle. Reassure a mortified Amy that's it's okay she forgot you don't like pickles; it's a hard day for everyone. Smile with your teeth and thank everyone for coming. Regret not cutting their brake lines when not a single one thanks you back.

This is what your husband says in the car on the way home.

*Those people were awful. I'm so sorry. Are you okay?*

This is what you say when he asks.

*I'm just glad that's over with.*

This is how to clean out an apartment.

Stand in the dimly-lit foyer, such as it is, and wonder how much jail time you'd get for arson. Think about going back to the car to cry. Decide against it, because Amy will be here in an hour, and you've got work to do. Open all the windows and doors, even though it's February, because if you don't, the yellow pall of cigarette smoke and death is going to give you a migraine. Turn on every light. Put on a pair of blue nitrile gloves and collect all the greasy ashtrays and unused medical consumables into a garbage bag; collect the contents of the fridge into a garbage bag. Collect the reeking pillows and blankets into a garbage bag. Stand in your dead father's bathroom, confronted with the soap scum, pubic hairs, and wrinkled stack of Hustler magazines that even at the end, even when he hadn't showered or peed independently in weeks, he still wouldn't let you clean up. Put on another pair of nitrile gloves. Reach for the dusty toilet brush and wonder why the fuck you even bother being alive.

These are the things that you find in your father's apartment.

Three unopened packs of Hanes crew socks. A cherry cough drop fused to a ten-year-old water bill. Seventeen dollars in change. Forty-three pesos in change. An empty condom box. An empty Altoids tin. An expired membership card for the NRA. A pair of red silk panties that most certainly weren't your mother's; a picture of the owner of said pant-ies, anonymous in her bold late-'80s perm, posing in an unidentifiable hotel room. Four loose Band-Aids, two of them used. The birthday card you sent your father last year, still unopened. The Father's Day card you sent him the year before, still unopened. A pack of stale cigarettes, which you throw in the trash but then fish back out, because you're not fifteen anymore and he's not here to punish you for stealing his smokes.

These are the things Amy finds.

A silver watch with your grandfather's initials. A bone-handled pocketknife with your grandfather's initials. A cream-colored wedding invitation with your parents' names printed in looping cursive. Your father's dog tags from Vietnam. His Purple Heart. A small plastic bag that contains three locks of baby hair. A palm-sized family photo that rockets you back to age seven, all five of you clean and smiling like models in a Sears catalog, with your mother's gentle handwriting on the back: *Stay alive for your children. All my love, Maggie.*

This is what Amy asks you when she finds the photo.

*Do you remember this?*

This is what you remember about the photo.

The languid October sun in your backyard. Fallen leaves crunching under your brand-new patent leather shoes purchased for your first day of second grade and carefully polished by your father to a mirror shine. Holding Amy up as she swayed against your knees, on the cusp of walking but not yet confident on her feet. The comforting scent of your mother's Coty Airspun powder as she pressed her cheek to yours. How you snuffled Adrian's neck for days afterward; your father's dense aftershave clinging to his soft baby skin.

This is what you remember about the day after the photo was taken.

Aunt Susan chain-smoking at the kitchen sink. Your father, chain-smoking at the kitchen table. Your mother holding a fussy Adrian and yelling at you to take Amy and go to your room, even though neither of you had done anything wrong. Pressing your ear to the crack under the door and listening to the grownups argue about how to pay for a trip to Canada that was never mentioned again.

This is what Amy asks when you don't answer.

*Were we really that happy?*

This is what you say when she asks.

*Are you really still working on the closet? Jesus Christ, Amy. The keys are due Friday.*

These are the people who come to take your father's unwanted things.

Eric, from the local VFA. Tansy, from the Union Gospel Mission. Rodolfo, Oscar and Luis from ALL-STAR JUNK REMOVAL. someone named Mike who might be a helpful neighbor or just a stranger who saw an opportunity for some fresh socks.

This is what you say to Adrian when your father's death certificate arrives.

*You're the lawyer. You do the paperwork.*

This is what you say when he starts to sob.

*Okay, okay, I'll take care of it.*

This is what Carl says to you when you punch End Call with a furious finger.

*I'll call my friend Judy. She did this for her husband last year and would love to help.*

These are the statistics for closing out your father's life.

One cup of coffee spilled on your laptop keyboard. Two hours at the DMV. Three different bank offices. $4000 for a disinterested estate attorney. Five months mired in probate. Six hours on hold with Social Security. Seven creditors trying to bully you into payment. Eight times you locked yourself in the bathroom and savagely bit down on a hand towel to scream. $9000 inheritance, split three ways. Ten allergy-inducing carnations in the large bouquet from your grateful younger siblings when you send them their checks.

This is what you've learned not to ask yourself.

*Haven't I done enough?*

Amy is the one to bring it up, mostly because I think Adrian finds her easier to talk to and more willing to broach difficult subjects than I am.

"What if we had a memorial?" she asks when we meet for drinks after she gets off work. "Something to mark the one-year anniversary?"

"We had a memorial."

"Yes, but something for *us*. Just us three." She offers a small, hopeful smile. "I think Adrian is ready to spread Dad's ashes, but he doesn't want to do it alone."

I take a sip of my IPA, savoring the shock of bitter hops. "So go with him."

"Marnie," Amy says, in that gentle tone that suggests I'm being unreasonable and grumpy again. "You don't have to, of course, but it would mean a lot if you were there."

Sometimes, it's easier to say *yes* than stand my ground, which is how I eventually find myself on the salt-worn deck of a cliffside Airbnb, watching as my younger siblings waffle at the shoreline below. Adrian has the wooden box in his hands, its lacquered surface flashing in the late-afternoon sun. Amy stands nearby, clinging to her fiancée Kitty's arm. I don't have to hear them to know that Adrian wants to heave the whole box into the surf—grand, impractical theatrics—while Amy is pointing out that it'll just float back with the tide, and shouldn't they pour the ashes into the water instead?

Carl comes up beside me, handing me a glass of Adrian's expensive merlot and pressing his shoulder against mine. "How's it going down there?"

"All that ash is going to blow back in their faces."

He snorts and raises his glass. "To your father, a selfish bastard even in death."

I clink my glass against his. "Cheers to that."

We stand in companionable silence, the pressure of his shoulder a calm counterpoint to the indecision on the beach. No one explicitly said I was the one who should care for our father when he was dying, but they didn't have to. If I went down to join my siblings now, they would immediately look to me for direction, ceding their own responsibility without question like they always have. I'd be put in charge whether or not I wanted it.

That's why I'm up here. Our father is dead. There is no higher authority over our generation now, no one to loom above and shame us into our familiar family roles. We are all equals now. I am done making their decisions. My therapist and I have been working hard on boundaries, and this is the most important one I need to declare.

Amy and Adrian roll up their pants and wade into the surf. I expect him to crumble as soon as the box is opened, but he doesn't, just holds it steady, his back to the horizon, as Amy removes the plastic bag that contains our father. She kneels and gently disperses our father, so he's caught by the water, not by the wind. Rising, she reaches for Adrian's hand and the two of them watch as the ashes swirl around their ankles.

I wonder if it bothers them that he's clinging to their skin. The thought of being marked by him in death, the microscopic shards of him digging into my pores and embedding in my lungs makes me want to vomit. I need to be free of him, to scrub away my obligations until the only remaining parts of him are the unremarkable fragments in my DNA.

I think I loved him once, and he loved me. He was the sort of father who polished my shoes, patiently guided me through Dick and Jane, and made sure my mother laughed every day. The war perverted him. It took a gentle man and turned him into someone inflexible and angry. As an adult, I understand the change wasn't entirely his fault, I *know* that, but I was also a child, betrayed and abandoned by someone I thought I knew.

Growing up, he always expected me to be someone better, someone kinder and more competent, someone who understood how to be a mother when Mom died and could raise his younger children when he didn't know how. I thought that if I could be all those things, if I tried hard enough, if I met that impossible standard, he would remember that he loved me.

I never could, and he never did.

As Amy and Adrian bring the empty box back to shore, Carl leans over to kiss my temple. "Hey," he says, his tone soft and concerned. "Penny for your thoughts?"

My siblings scuff their feet in the sand. The box that contained our father is now five pounds lighter, a lightness that suddenly echoes like a drum in my chest. He's gone; his physical self dispersed among the foam. There is only one thing to say, a heady truth that has nothing to do with the wine.

"I'm free," I say, and then giddy tears spill over. "For the first time in my life, I'm actually free."

I know how to be the eldest daughter. Now, I get to learn how to be myself.

# LOVE NOTE FOR THINGS NEVER COMING AGAIN

*Poem by Randy Bynum*

This night is all Chablis and timbre,
a diamond-studded black belt dojo
ready to shower you to the ground
proving you are not so important.

A coyote walks by, looking for hope
or just following the sound of owls.

I could hear momma at her stove
over a mile away in the tilted cabin,
cooking and singing an old hymn,
stoking the iron-bellied fire with love.

She's been dead for years, decades,
and not able to tend a fresh garden
the way she wants, myrrh and thyme
waiting to be reincarnated as doves.

I start dreaming, standing up, looking
for beloveds, mist-cloaked and soaked
in dustbowl memory, unpeeling artichoke
leaves and pages, under a despot's gaze.

That coyote dances now, wondering if we
had prayed or were prey, blending to brown

mortal night. Nothing comes of nothing, oh
King Lear's so right. Momma comes out, tells
him to quit that posturing, get washed up, then
come eat dinner. Her Cherokee blood is glowing.

# TRIBUTE TO THE WAR RAGING IN MY HEAD

*Visual art by Adamu Yahuza Abdullahi*

# HIGHER

*Poem by Scott Bigger*

Standing at this window,
I rest my hands
      on limestone
and lean over the edge
to gaze
      like a voyeur
into wet twilight.

High up here,
I can see the place where my mother
fell, and
bloodied her nose,
blackened her eyes,
      and broke out teeth.
Her balance was gone.
Her vigor
      gone
      in only one short year
      in a short lifetime
of medical bills and hospital visits.

Some of those sterile rooms
      had windows
      like this.

I'm sure
if I grabbed the frame
and got my knees up on the fitted blocks
      and

felt the edge work its way through
fabric to flesh,
          that from here
I could see
where the wind knocked over the big oak
          in the corner of the field
late last year
like a heavy blow from an open hand
to knock
          a child
to the ground.

The carcass of the tree
picked clean
in days
          for firewood
like the memory of an old horse
decaying
out in the grass.

The stone is solid.
I know that
              if
I stand on the sill
I can see even farther
like I could from my father's shoulders
when I was so much younger.

Higher,
and I could probably see the gate
          at the end of the pasture.

Driving the tractor
      alone in the field
      on a rainy evening like this,
      I knew I was too high
but that
      once
I reached the corner gate
the power lines would be higher still,

and I'd be
      safe
from the lightning,
      home and dry.

Now
      I crouch in the window
      and peer into the darkening sky.

They say
      farming is the most hazardous occupation.
They say
      the family farm is disappearing.

Dad lived his life in that space
      between taking his wife to doctor's appointments
      and taking the golden disappointment
      of thin wheat
      in off the field;
the weight of it crushed him from the outside in
      like a truck box full of withered kernels
      falling like a beam of light
stretched out in the slow flickering motion
      of years.

For Mom,
        the bone and marrow and blood
of that life
        ate her up from the inside out
        like cells boiling out from hiding,
and it couldn't kill her fast enough.
        A few beats,
        a few days,
a couple of empty weeks,
and the strange heart beats no more.

Smooth from years
and slick from tears
        of rain,
water runs
        down the rock header of the window,
        to slide down my face,
to drip
        and vanish in the falling dusk.

In the window,
        in this vacant square of vision
I frame my life:

I can never seem to get high enough,
        to see them
                anymore,
so far from the farm,
no longer home,
        not mine,
        not theirs either.

In this frame,
I push myself to stand up,
to let go,
          to step
back.

# THE PAINTER

*Fiction by Gretchen Keefer*

I was disinterestedly poking around in a resale/antique/junk shop with a friend, and I was not seeing anything I wanted to spend my money on, but when I glanced around, a jumble of color caught my eye. Reaching the shelf, what caught my eye turned out to be a plastic bag of small bird houses brightly painted in reds, yellows, greens and blues. The tiny wooden boxes with the sloped roof and small hole in one side looked familiar. I turned the collection around until I came to a painted bottom panel. There I found a small red "I" with distinctive flourishes on the top and bottom lines. Inez. This is where some of her things ended up. Nothing else in the store looked like it had been hers. My companion was ready to leave. I grabbed the package of bird houses, paid, and left.

Inez.

I remembered when I first met Inez. Dressed in a paint-covered smock, paintbrush in her hand, she greeted me at the door with a cheery hello. Transferring the paint brush to her mouth, she deftly steered her wheelchair into the sparsely furnished room, stopping at a worktable with an easel, paints and brushes within easy reach. The room was in disarray, but the worktable looked well organized. "Come in", she called as she moved. "You can put your things on that chair. Let's get acquainted."

That was one of the most enjoyable hours I have spent with a client. Inez spoke about her art, pointing out a couple of the paintings on the wall as hers. They were large red and yellow flowers growing in a garden. They looked familiar; when I said so, Inez laughed. She told me a similar painting was hanging in the lobby of the apartment building. She mentioned some other local landmark buildings where her paintings were hanging. I was impressed. I was working with a real artist.

The painting in progress was a smaller watercolor version of the garden, the red and yellow flowers accented with bright green leaves. Inez admitted she could no longer handle the large canvases, nor paint in oils.

"The paint tubes are too difficult to squeeze the paint from. And," she sighed, "I don't have the time. The Cancer is rushing me." She always spoke of her illness as *The Cancer*, her nemesis of the last twenty years. Often, she had beaten the disease, only to have it pop up somewhere else in her body two or three years later. Once her remission lasted over six years. "That's when I married Number Two. We thought everything would be all right." Inez smiled. "But I will win in the end. The Cancer cannot stop me from making the world more beautiful."

Inez's bouncy personality was larger than her physical frame and spilled over onto her canvases. She was short and slightly pudgy, her black hair streaked with white, her dark eyes sparking with good humor. Her paintings were full of life and color. Flowers were her favorite subject. She also painted playing children, happy dogs and soaring trees. Sometimes the trees soared over a garden of red, yellow, and blue flowers and a small girl picking them with her little brown puppy at her heels.

When we went to her appointments, we generally planned additional time to visit the city gardens and admire whatever was in season. If there was an art exhibit at the city hall or community center, we visited it as well. Inez always had a kind word to say about the artist or the work, even if it was not to her liking. One time we visited an installation of light boxes. I was not impressed with the rectangular shapes, covered with colored plexiglass and provided with a light bulb inside. Inez sat thoughtfully in her chair for a long time, then pronounced the artist as "trying to help people see color in their world".

About a year after I started visiting Inez, she traded her wheelchair in for a power-driven model since she could no longer maneuver the standard chair in her apartment. The push type wheelchair was available for outings, which became fewer and fewer. Inez also became heavier and more spread out. Fitting into the conventional chair was a challenge. "Ah, The Cancer is squishing me," she explained, "like flattening a meatball into a meat patty. He hasn't beaten me yet!"

"He?" I queried. "You made your cancer male?"

"Yes. Anyone who has ever hurt me was male—both husbands, some boyfriends, my brother, an uncle. Yes, male. So," she laughed, "I get back at them."

One day her son and his wife came to visit while I was on shift. Knowing they probably had business to discuss (he had only once before come during the day), I busied myself in the kitchen, cleaning the refrigerator. Inez was eating less; there were many leftovers to sort through. All her caregivers were good about dating food in the fridge, but not as ready to serve it to her again. The daughter-in-law wandered through, looking bored. She scanned the paintings on the walls, flipped through the watercolor sketch book and sighed. "My husband thinks his mother is a great artist. It's all very garish and childish, isn't it? What could you do with all this paper?"

I told her the watercolors could be matted and sold. In Inez's defense I mentioned the major local buildings where her paintings were displayed. "An original Inez Villareal could become quite valuable." She looked around, shrugged her shoulders, and wandered back to the conversation in the bedroom.

Inez was no longer painting on canvases, nor trying to frame her work. Her watercolors filled pages of art tablets in decreasing size. Occasionally she didn't finish a painting for a few weeks. One day when I arrived, she greeted me with a friendly *good morning* and remained quiet for several minutes staring at the unfinished painting on the table. The painting lacked her usual color and zest. One could imagine a dying garden—a radical change for Inez. I brought her a clean glass of water for her brushes. "Sit," she said, pointing to the chair. I sat.

"The paintings are gone. I think I am finishing my work."

"Gone? Where?"

"Out of my head. I could see images, so I painted them. I don't see them now. I feel like my time is nearly up." She turned to face me. "The doctors agree with me. Just a couple of months, they say."

I skipped a beat or two trying to find a response to this statement. "Does this bother you?"

"Oh, no. I am not afraid to die. I've been there before." Inez then told me about an out-of-body experience she had a few years ago during a procedure at the hospital. "It was beautiful—so warm, friendly, loving there. I wanted to stay. There were some children. One little girl reached out her hand to me. I know if I had taken it, I would have stayed."

"What happened?"

Inez sighed. "The doctor called me back." The Inez sparkle was back in her eyes, and she giggled slightly. "I'm afraid I was rude to him. I answered 'Wha-a-a-t?'" She paused. "I'm just afraid of the pain. And I must keep painting. I will not let The Cancer take that from me."

Inez soon found something else to paint. One of her other caregivers brought in an unfinished balsa wood model of a VW bus. The watercolors were exchanged for acrylic craft paint. The internet was searched, and more bare wood items were found. Soon Inez was spreading her joyful colors on toy cars, airplanes, a barn or two, and small birdhouses. Most of the finished items were given away. We all helped her by sharing the joy with our friends.

* * *

I held the bundle of little birdhouses in my hand. They were too fragile to hang in a tree, exposed to the weather. And too tiny for the birds. Perhaps a hummingbird could enter the hole, but they don't nest in boxes. The houses could be a lovely spot of color on a patio wall or nestled in a spring wreath on the front door. I thought a long time about Inez and the joy she tried to share by coloring the world. Then I got to work.

I'm not much of a crafter, but I could glue a few pieces of lace or braid on the painted birdhouses and give them away. Enough names came to mind of people who needed a jolt of cheer to find homes for all the birdhouses I had found that day in the shop. I started to look for more of Inez's work.

* * *

It was a different resale shop. I knew as soon as I saw the big red blossoms in the watercolor that it was Inez's work. It wasn't easy to find her small signature *I*. The matte had covered it, but it was there. I knelt in the aisle by the shelf, holding the painting in my hands and trying to visualize it in every room of my home, unsuccessfully. Regretfully I put the painting back on the shelf.

"Oh, good," I heard a woman exclaim behind me. "Are you not going to take that painting? I've been looking all over for something affordable and colorful to decorate the bare white walls in my apartment. This is just the right size. And it is so bright and cheerful." The woman started to walk away with the red blossoms tucked under her arm.

"I knew the artist," I called after her. She stopped, curious. I told her all I knew about Inez's success as a painter and showed her how to find the *I* to verify the authenticity.

She grinned, pleased to have more information about her new piece of art, something she could brag about. "Thank you. So, I have an original Inez Villareal. An original piece of genuine art. Wow."

Inez is still spreading joy.

# THE PROMISE

*Poem by Joshua Bott*

Dahlias, poetic as they are,
still decompose as quickly as most other flora.

And while related to the sunflower, the chrysanthemum, and the daisy,
this relation does not belabor their decaying.

I've got a sense that love is a dahlia.
As beautiful and poetic as it is,
time will wear it like a spendthrift's sweater.

And that what we are promised is not what we imagined it would be.
And who the promise is for, and who has made the promise,
nameless and unquantifiable as sea foam.

# CONTRIBUTORS

**ADAMU YAHUZA ABDULLAHI,** THE PLOB, TPC V, MAAR II, is a poet and visual artist from Borgu, Nigeria. His debut poetry collection, *The Rainbow is Not As Beautiful as my Ruins*, is forthcoming from Felis Catus Press.

**SCOTT BIGGER** grew up on a farm in northern Minnesota before pursuing a career writing software in the Pacific Northwest. In addition to having previously published poetry, his fiction has been recognized with a Kay Snow award. He now lives in Portland, Oregon, with his wife, two cats, and a dog, where he writes about ordinary people in extraordinary circumstances.

**LISA BISHOP** is a lifelong story-dweller, currently nestled in Portland, Oregon. She is delighted to discover that her jumble of career paths, world travels, and unruly imagination can (indeed) transform into entertaining tales. Her curiosity compels her to read ancient myths, the latest developments in quantum theory, and everything in between. She volunteers for Willamette Writers and has co-founded international art and wellness workshops. Her experiences with parenting, mental health, and the writing life are shared on Medium and Substack. On any given day, Lisa can be found wandering downtown with her husband, listening to pop punk classics, or pocketing a random rock.

**JOSHUA BOTT** is an educator and poet who lives in Portland, Oregon with his partner and their cat, Scout. He grew up in Coos Bay, Oregon before attending Linfield University, where he studied poetry and philosophy. He has lived in the Portland area since 2008 and received a master's in education from Portland State University in 2019. Joshua is an active member of the Portland nonprofit group Literary Arts and enjoys supporting youth poetry and helping poets find their voice in

Oregon's vibrant literary community. In addition to writing, Joshua enjoys playing disc golf, listening to a wide variety of strange music, and playing unnecessarily long board games with friends.

**TRICIA GATES BROWN**'s poetry has appeared in *Portland Review*, *ANTAE Journal*, and *Yellow Arrow Journal*, among other publications, and her first poetry collection *Of A Certain Age* is forthcoming from Fernwood Press in mid-2025. By trade, she is an editor and co-writer, mainly working for the National Park Service and Native tribes. Her debut novel *Wren* won a 2022 Independent Publishers Award Bronze Medal. For fun, she makes art.

**PIXIE BRUNER** (HWA/SFPA) is a writer, editor, and cancer survivor. She is *Pushcart* nominated and the 2025 Rhysling Award Chair. She lives in Atlanta, GA, with her *doppelgänger*. Her words are in the Elgin-nominated "The Body As Haunted" (Authortunities Press), *Space & Time Magazine*, *Weird Fiction Quarterly*, and many more.

**RANDY BYNUM**'s work appears in *The Good Life Review* (2024 Honeybee Prize Winner for Poetry), *Cirque* (2023 contest winner), *Arboreal Literary Magazine*, *Metonym Journal*, *Atticus Review*, *New Plains Review*, *Cathexis Northwest Press*, *Santa Clara Review*, *Clackamas Literary Review*, *Cutthroat*, and others. His mother, ½ Native American/Cherokee who hid it until late in life, inspired him. Collections seeking publication: *Tulips Talking Behind My Back* and four volumes of magical realism entitled *Dragons Who Type: Poems of Whimsy and Wishes*. He's an award-winning playwright, ("The Convert", Kennedy Center/ ACTF, Region IX), living in Oregon with wife Dani and rescue dog Coop.

**DOUG EMORY** is a freelance writer and educational consultant, who lives with his wife and younger son near Seattle. He is the author of a forthcoming short story collection from *Iron Horse Literary Review*, and his full range of publications is broad, including a textbook on college writing, a hiking guidebook, and numerous articles on climbing, cross-country skiing, and mountaineering culture. His short stories and adventure narratives have won major writing competitions and been published in premier national climbing magazines such as *Rock and Ice* and *Alpinist*.

**JOE MICHAEL FEIST** grew up in hot West Texas where he endured nuns and nosy neighbors in a land that was mostly sky. He loved his grandmother's kolaches, drank heavily and worked in the fields. Feist earned two degrees, including a Master of Arts in history, from Texas A&M University. He settled on a career messin' with words, first writing and editing for Catholic publications, then for secular newspapers such as his beloved *Dallas Morning News*. Feist ended his working days playing with words at various universities. Now retired, he breathes in San Antonio where he writes frantically, eats kolaches, drinks heavily and loves a land that is mostly sky. He no longer works in the fields.

**ANNE MARIE FOWLER** holds a Ph.D. in world literature in English and translation and an MFA in poetry. Her creative work has been published nationally and internationally, most recently in *Black Fox Literary Magazine* and *Good River Review*. Creatively, she seeks to understand the magic of nature, the defining characteristics that make humans operate, and the connectivity of experience between and within cultures. When not writing, she plays hard at being retired.

**GRETCHEN KEEFER** often writes (or rewrites) scenes and dialog in her head for fun. Connecting with Writers in the Grove in Forest Grove, Oregon, helped to fine tune her writing and encouraged her to start submitting her stories. Gretchen's short stories focus on the positive and, sometimes, the whimsical. She feels there is always some good to be found. Now retired to Tillamook, Gretchen continues to submit short stories and is working on a short young adult novel. Her work has appeared on *CommuterLit.com, ArielChart.com, The Academy of the Heart and Mind,* and in *Rain Magazine, Chicken Soup for the Soul, Particular Passages: Decked Halls, Voices from the Millpond,* and other anthologies.

**RICK LEVIN** is an award-winning journalist turned bus driver living in Eugene, Oregon. His work has appeared in *The Stranger, The Seattle Weekly* and *The Eugene Weekly,* among other publications.

**ALIYU UMAR MUHAMMAD** is a Nigerian poet, literary coach, digital artist and secretary, Muktar Aliyu Art Residency Minna, Nigeria. He has work forthcoming in *Consequence Forum Magazine, Sunlight Press Magazine, Shooter Lit Magazine* and elsewhere. Aliyu was longlisted for Idumaese Alao prize for literature 2024 and Abubakar Gimba's prize for creative non-fiction 2023. He is a fellow at Ebedi International Writer's Residency. Aliyu resides in Minna and finds peace in rhythms and aesthetics of art.

**EVE MÜLLER** lives in Eugene, Oregon with her sweetheart. She has recently published in *Camas, Cirque, Empty House, Marrow Magazine, Sea Wolf Journal, Sequestrum, Thieving Magpie,* and *The Writing Disorder.* Some of her work has been anthologized, and her first book, *Guide to the Ruins,* was published by Plan B Press, with a second book, *Birds and Saints,* forthcoming. She was awarded a PLAYA artists' residency this year, and her work was nominated for a Pushcart Prize. When Eve is not writing, she bakes, hikes, conducts research on autism, hangs out with her mom and two feral daughters, and skinny-dips whenever/ wherever she can.

Over the years, **SUE PACE**'s poetry, prose and personal essays have been published in Australia, the UK and the USA. She often says, "Writing is the most selfish thing I do."

Looking at the world through a camera lens allows **KITT PATTEN** to see wonders that she might otherwise have missed.  Her quest is to capture these moments so she can share their beauty with others. Her photography has been published in *Shots* magazine, *The North Coast Squid,* and previous issues of *the Timberline Review,* and can be seen online at *The Sunlight Press* and in issue number 31 of the *3Elements Literary Review.*

**CHRISTIAN PAULISICH** graduated from Johns Hopkins University, where he worked on *The Hopkins Review.* He works as a therapist in Northern Maryland, but is originally from the Bay Area, California. He was recently chosen as an honorable mention for the 2024 Gulf Coast Prize for Poetry and a finalist for *Frontier Poetry's* 2024 Nature & Place Contest and received a Summer 2024 fellowship from *Brooklyn Poets.* His work has been published in or is forthcoming from *The Southeast Review, Salamander, Frontier, Literary Matters, Crab Orchard Review, Denver Quarterly,* and other magazines. He currently reads poetry submissions for *Palette Poetry.*

**PATRICK T. REARDON,** a five-time nominee in poetry for the Pushcart Prize, was a *Chicago Tribune* reporter for 32 years. His latest poetry collection *Every Marred Thing: A Time in America,* the winner of the 2024 Faulkner-Wisdom Prize from the Pirate's Alley Faulkner Society of New Orleans, was published in April 2025, by Lavender Ink. He has published six other collections, including *Requiem for David* (Silver Birch) and *Puddin': The Autobiography of a Baby, A Memoir in Prose Poems* (Third World Press).

**BRIAN ROHR** is a poet, writer, and performative storyteller based in Beaverton, OR. He is the founder and director of *The Stafford Challenge,* an international poetry project inspired by the legendary William Stafford, which has encouraged over a thousand participants to write a poem every day for a year. His writing has appeared in *Blink Ink, The Words Faire*, the *Jewish Literary Journal*, along with several anthologies. As a storyteller and performative poet, Rohr has taught and performed at major conferences, high schools, universities, synagogues, libraries, and in solo concerts. His debut book, *Shaken to My Bones: A Poetic Midrash on the Torah*, was published by Ben Yehuda Press in 2024. His work explores mythology, mysticism, ecology, and the transformative power of story.  Learn more at  brianrohr.com | staffordchallenge.com

**CHRISTOPHER RUBIO-GOLDSMITH** was born in Merida, Yucatan, grew up in Tucson, Arizona and taught English at Tucson High School for 27 years. Much of his work explores growing up near the border, being raised biracial/bilingual and teaching in a large urban school where 70% of the students are American/Mexican. An Allen Ginsberg Poetry Award Honorable Mention, a two-time Pushcart nominee, and winner of the Eleventh-Hour Poetry Contest. His wife Kelly lets him know when the writing is off a bit. He is trying to get better at sitting and seeing.

**CRAIG ("C.M.") SELBREDE** is a recent graduate of Bates College in Lewiston, Maine. A Maryland native, he is best known for his self-published works, including the *Valley Chronicles* trilogy and National Gold Medal winner *Makeshift*, but has also co-created Unthank Productions' fantasy web series *Relic* and dramedy web series *Hurt*. Craig enjoys telling stories that transcend genre and convention to cut to the heart of humanity.

**KAT TABOR** is an artist and journalist studying at Lane Community College, who serves as Editor-in-Chief of *The Torch*, a student-run newspaper. An intern reporter at *Eugene Weekly*, Kat's creative work spans visual art, photography, and writing—all of which reflect deep passion for storytelling and life. Kat's art often explores themes of female resistance in the face of adversity, using creativity as a tool for empowerment.

**COLETTE TENNANT** has three books of poetry: *Commotion of Wings*, *Eden and After*, and *Sweet Gothic*. Her book, *Religion in The Handmaid's Tale: a Brief Guide*, was published in 2019 to coincide with Atwood's publication of *The Testaments*. Her poems have won various awards and have been nominated for Pushcart Prizes along with being published in various journals, including *Prairie Schooner*, *Rattle*, *Southern Poetry Review*, and *Poetry Ireland Review*. Colette is an English and Humanities Professor who has also taught art in Great Britain, Germany, and Italy.

**JAIMEE WALLS** writes essays and short stories and has been published in the *VanCougar*, *Columbia River Reader*, and *The Sun Magazine*. Her work can also be found on NW-Scribes.com. She is working on her first sci-fi fantasy novel and is the happily overworked webmaster of the Southwest Washington Writers Conference. When not writing, she enjoys reading obsessively, old-school roller skating, attempting to snuggle with her antisocial cats, participating in critique groups or anything writing-related, building websites, and troubleshooting and resolving stubborn computer issues.

**KR WOODRUFF** (she/her) is a novelist whose work focuses on relationships, identity, and the messy business of being human. A passionate SFF fan, mental health advocate, and gardener, she currently lives in Portland, Oregon, with her husband and two fluffy black cats.

**KYLIE YOUNG** writes about nature, gendered labor, and the history of science. She lives in Oregon with her husband and cat.

**AMANDA YSKAMP**'s work has appeared in such magazines as *Threepenny Review*, *Hayden Review*, *Caketrain*, *Redivider*, and *The Georgia Review*. She lives on the 10-year flood plain of the Russian River and teaches writing from her online schoolhouse.

# BLACKBIRD WHISTLING

IN BLACKBIRD WHISTLING, DIAN GREENWOOD WEAVES A MASTERFUL STORY OF INTERGENERATIONAL TRAUMA THROUGH THE EYES OF A GRANDMOTHER AND HER GRANDDAUGHTER. TOGETHER, THEY FIND THEIR WAY BACK TO THEMSELVES AND EACH OTHER.

FIND OUT MORE AT DIANGREENWOOD.COM/

## BY DIAN GREENWOOD

# I KNOW ABOUT THESE THINGS

"JACOBI WEAVES HER WORDS INTO POEMS, USING OLD PHOTOGRAPHS, EVENTS, AND STORIES, AS WELL AS HER OWN LIVED EXPERIENCES, ALL OF WHICH PULL AT THE READER'S EMOTION AND IMAGINATION. SHE TELLS THE TRUTH, HER TRUTH. INDEED, SHE DOES KNOW ABOUT THESE THINGS."
ANITA JANIS, REVIEWER

## BY CYNTHIA JACOBI

# THE BEST I CAN DO

SHE STARTED OFF HAPPY, SUCCESSFUL, AND LOOKING FORWARD TO THE FUTURE.

SO HOW DID SHE END UP HOMELESS AND BROKE?

FIND OUT MORE AT TABBYCATCO.COM/

## BY CHERYL LANDES

# LOOK UP, GIRL!

THIS 100-DAY DEVOTIONAL IS SPECIFICALLY DESIGNED FOR WOMEN STRUGGLING WITH FEAR, WORRY, AND SELF-DESTRUCTIVE THINKING. PERFECT FOR THOSE FIGHTING ANXIETY, THIS GOD-CENTERED MATERIAL OFFERS ENCOURAGEMENT TO READERS SEARCHING FOR THE BRIGHTER SIDE OF LIFE.

## BY KIMBERLY SHUMATE

VOLUNTEER WITH
WILLAMETTE WRITERS
VOLUNTEERS MAKE OUR PROGRAMMING POSSIBLE

HANG OUT WITH
WILLAMETTE WRITERS
JOIN US AT THE WILLAMETTE WRITERS CONFERENCE

CONNECT
WITH
WILLAMETTE
WRITERS
MEET INDUSTRY PROFESSIONALS
AND COLLEAGUES

SET GOALS
WITH
WILLAMETTE
WRITERS
ONLINE PRODUCTIVITY MEETING
EVERY THURSDAY AT NOON

# HAVE COFFEE WITH

# WILLAMETTE WRITERS



# WRITE WITH

9 789898 642251